For Emery

A Sports Romance

J. NATHAN

Edited by Stephanie Elliot
Cover Design by Letitia Hasser at RBA Designs
Cover Photo by Fabrice Lerouge

First Edition February 2019

CHAPTER ONE

Grady

I haven't always been a prick...

Age 11

Darkness filled my room as I lay in bed. The tape on my football posters had peeled off and the curled bottoms flapped in the late October breeze seeping through my open window.

"I'll kill you, you bitch," a deep voice carried across our lawn from the home of our new neighbors. They'd arrived a week ago. And not once since the small moving van pulled up, had there been any silence coming from their home at night.

"Hello?"

The small whisper jarred me upright. I might've only been eleven, but hearing voices was definitely something new for me.

The quiet plea repeated. "Hello?"

I crept out from under my sheets and crawled to the window beside my bed. I could only see the top of the blonde-haired girl who stood outside.

"You okay?" I asked, pushing my window up until it was all the way open.

Her head tilted up. Her big blue eyes, puffy with tears, met mine. She shook her head. "Can I come in?" she sniffled.

My eyes shot behind me at my closed bedroom door. Would my parents be angry if I let her in? I mean, I didn't even know her name. "Ummmm…"

Noticing my indecision, she turned away. "Never mind."

Shoot. "Wait."

She stopped but didn't turn around.

"Sure. Fine. You can come in."

She spun around and scurried over. She couldn't have been more than four feet. I reached for her to help her up, and she placed the tiniest hands I'd ever seen into my oversized bear claws. "How old are you?" I asked, lifting her through my window as if she weighed nothing at all.

She dropped onto her knees on my bed. "Eight." Her eyes moved over my room. It was your average eleven-year-old boy's room. "Wow."

The awe in her voice embarrassed me. I knew the house she'd moved into was kind of a dump, so I understood her amazement at the size of my room. I reached for the window and closed it, not wanting her to hear her parents' loud voices. Though I'd overheard my mom say it wasn't her real dad. "What's your name?"

"Emery Pruitt," she drawled, her accent as thick as my momma's molasses.

"Good to meet you, Emery Pruitt."

She smiled through her teary eyes. "You, too, Jordan Grady."

"How'd you know my name?"

She quickly wiped her damp cheeks with the back of her hand. "I have my ways."

I laughed at this little eight-year-old who was likely tougher than my entire football team. You had to be to deal with the amount of fighting her parents did. "So, what shall we do?" I asked, suddenly feeling completely unequipped to help her.

"Sleep," she said. "I just need to sleep."

I scooted off the edge of my twin bed until my bare feet hit the hardwood floor and pulled back the sheet. "Here."

Emery climbed underneath and tucked herself into a ball. She was so tiny in my bed. Such a wounded little soul who probably hadn't gotten a lick of sleep since moving in.

"Whatcha waiting for?" she asked. "Hop in."

"I'm gonna take the floor."

She scrunched her perky little nose. "Why?"

I shrugged.

She rolled over as far as she could, leaving a huge space for me. "Come on. I promise not to kick you in the middle of the night."

I snickered to myself as my eyes shifted between the uncomfortable floor and my cozy bed. It was a no brainer. I climbed in beside her. We both fell silent, laying on our backs and staring up at the ceiling fan spinning above us.

"Thank you, Jordan Grady," she whispered.

"You're welcome, Emery Pruitt."

It took no more than two minutes before the soft purr of her snores filled my room.

* * *

I awoke the next morning to a wide-open window and an empty spot beside me. I reached over and smoothed my hand over the cold sheets, wondering how long Emery had stayed. Had her parents noticed she'd disappeared? Had she walked in to them waiting for her in the kitchen?

The smell of homemade pancakes from my own kitchen drifted into my room. I rolled out of bed and padded down the hallway with my bare feet. Scrubbing my hands over my face, I entered the kitchen. My parents sat at the table where a stack of pancakes filled the plate in front of my chair. "Morning," I said, slipping into my seat.

"Morning, honey," my mom said, sipping her coffee.

My dad didn't look up from his newspaper. "Morning, son."

"Your practice was moved to this evening," my mom said.

I glanced to my mom as I stuffed a forkful of pancakes into my mouth. "Why?"

"With the heatwave moving through town, your coaches feel it'll be more bearable once the sun begins to set."

I nodded, realizing they had no idea I'd had a visitor the previous night. "Can I ask you something?" I said.

My mom lowered her coffee cup. "Sure."

"Any idea what happened to the little girl next door's real daddy?"

My dad folded up his paper. "Why do you ask?"

"I just assumed you guys would know," I said, stuffing more pancakes into my mouth.

"I heard he died of cancer while her mother was pregnant with her," my mom admitted sadly.

I nodded, my stomach clenching for Emery.

"Why are you so curious all of a sudden?" my dad asked.

I shrugged. "There's a lot of yellin' goin' on over there. I wondered what makes people fight like that?"

My parents exchanged a sad look. "Unhappiness I assume," my mom said before changing the subject to the weather—a safer topic to discuss with her eleven-year-old son.

After breakfast, I ran outside, tossing my football above my head and catching it as it dropped into my hands. When we didn't have practice, my friends and I normally met at the park for a game then we hit the creek to cool off before playing another game. I threw another spiral above my head.

"Hey."

I twisted around and the football dropped on my head, tumbling unceremoniously to the ground.

"Looks like someone needs practice," Emery said as she skipped toward me, her blonde hair in a high ponytail that was swinging from side to side.

I bent and nabbed the ball, spinning it in my hands. "Says who?"

"Says me."

"What makes you a professional on the subject?"

She shrugged. "Toss it to me."

I shuffled back a few feet and threw her a perfect spiral. She bobbled it in her hands and dropped it. "Looks like someone needs more practice," I teased.

She bent and grabbed the ball from the lawn. "Then I'm glad you live next door," she said without missing a beat. She clearly didn't plan to talk about the previous night, and that was fine by me. I wasn't a therapist. I didn't know the right things to say to someone who had a drunk for a stepdad.

I held up my hands. "Throw it here."

She tossed a wobbly pass to me which I caught easily.

"You're gonna want to line up your fingertips on the laces," I said, showing her my hand on the football. "Then just let it roll off your fingers." I tossed it to her in a perfect spiral which she bobbled with both hands but held on to it. "Nice catch."

She smiled. "Thanks."

"Now you try."

She lined up her fingers like I'd shown her. She pulled back her hand and let it go. The ball carried straighter than her last pass, though her spiral needed some work.

"Not bad," I assured her.

"You really think so?"

"Yup."

"Do you play football every day?" she asked.

"Yup. I need to practice if I'm gonna play for Alabama one day."

That was her cue to laugh. Everyone else did. I was used to it by now. No one thought I'd make it—except of course my parents. But then again, they thought I hung the moon, so it didn't count. "Can I come to your games?" Emery asked.

I shrugged. "If you want to. They're every Saturday at the field by the park."

She shook her head. "No. When you play for Alabama." She wasn't laughing at me. She wasn't even humoring me. She really believed me when I said I'd play for Alabama.

I smiled. "Sure."

"Can I have a front-row seat?"

"Absolutely."

"I'm gonna be your biggest fan, Jordan Grady. You just wait and see."

I laughed, because something in the way she said it, told me it was the truth.

"Whatcha waiting for?" she asked. "If you're gonna play for Alabama, you need some serious practice." The little smart ass held up her hands.

I tossed her the ball, easier this time so she could catch it without bobbling it. She did. "Nice catch."

She tilted her head. "You ain't seen nothing yet."

"No?"

She shook her head.

And somehow, I believed that too.

CHAPTER TWO

Grady - 15

I lay in bed with my arms crossed behind my head, my mind whirling with indecision. Shyanne and Miley both wanted me to ask them to the school dance. They'd been causing unnecessary scenes at school all week. And there was nothing I hated more than girl drama. Did I even want to go to some lame-ass dance? High school girls were so…different. I just wanted a girl who'd jump in the creek with me on the count of one. One who'd toss around a football without groaning about breaking a nail. One who'd believe me when I said I was gonna play football at Alabama.

Someone like Emery.

The guys had been busting my balls for the past four years about my "little shadow." But I didn't care. I knew the truth about our friendship. I knew the truth about her family life. I knew the truth about our bond. Besides, I liked my "little shadow" a hell of a lot more than most of them.

"Leave! Just leave!" Emery's mom's voice carried through the night. She threatened her husband all the time. But he never left. He just drank more.

I hated the idea of Emery living in that house. She assured me Wayne had never hurt her. And despite her assurances, I repeatedly begged my parents to call the sheriff. When they'd had enough of me asking—and I assumed hearing all the fighting—they called him. He stopped by Emery's house while she was at school. But Emery's mom told him everything was fine. Because of her unwillingness to report domestic violence, the sheriff told my parents there was nothing he could do.

I felt helpless.

I'd always been told if you didn't like something that was happening, you needed to do something to stop it. But aside from killing Emery's stepdad, there wasn't anything I could do but give Emery a safe place to escape to.

The tapping on my window came like clockwork. I didn't even go to the window anymore. At twelve, Emery was tall enough to push it up herself, climb inside, close the window behind her, and crank up my ceiling fan to drown out the unwanted noise. "Hi," she whispered as she crawled under my sheet and turned on her side away from me.

"You okay?"

"I am now."

My heart squeezed in my chest. The girl would be the death of me. "How was school today?" I asked, trying to redirect her attention from the fight.

"Same. How was yours?" she asked.

Thoughts of Shyanne and Miley fighting over me plagued my mind. "Same."

"You're lying," Emery said.

"How do you know?"

"You paused."

"So?"

"So, you pause when you're not saying somethin'."

I huffed. Of course she could tell I had something on my mind. She knew me better than anyone. "A couple girls want me to ask them to the school dance."

Emery's body stiffened and a long moment passed before she spoke. "And?"

"And…I don't know what to do?"

"What to do or who to ask?"

"Both."

You could've cut the silence in my room with a knife, hacksaw, *and* axe. "You could just take me and not have to worry about it," she finally said.

I scoffed. "Right."

She spun and faced me, anger blazing in her eyes. "What's that mean?"

Even though she was adorable when she was angry, I knew better than to smile. "You're twelve. This is a high school dance."

"I'll be in high school in a few years."

"But you're not now," I said.

"Yes. You remind me of that fact daily."

I stared into her eyes. Hurt replaced the anger, which just made me feel like shit. I had no idea what else to say to make her feel better. I knew she had a crush on me. If she was my age, I may have been crushing on her too. But she wasn't. End of story.

The silence in the room carried her parents' fight inside. "You son of a bitch! Who is she?"

Emery's eyes cut to the window.

Oh, damn. It was bad enough she had a drunk for a stepdad, she didn't need to hear he was a cheat, too.

"Do you even know how to dance?" I asked, trying to redirect her attention.

Her eyes moved back to mine. "Of course I know how to dance."

"I've never seen you."

She shoved me playfully. "Whose fault is that?"

"She takes care of my needs!" Emery's stepdad yelled, seemingly in the front yard now.

Emery's body wilted.

I reached out and pulled her small body into my chest. She came willingly. I pressed my lips to the top of her head, not really knowing what to do or say. She was just a kid. And I was just a stupid teenager. My mind was normally on sports and sex for Christ's sake.

"I'm never gonna drink alcohol," she whispered into my chest.

"Good. It messes with your judgment."

"How do you know?" she asked.

"Just do."

She was quiet for a long time. Luckily, only the crickets chirping outside my house carried their way inside now. "And I never wanna fight like that when I get married," she added.

"Then don't."

"I won't," she assured me. "I'm only gonna give my heart to a boy who'll love me and never wanna fight with me."

"Who do you think you'll marry? Billy Rae?"

She hauled off and punched me in the gut.

"Ow!" I said, feeling a sharp pain emanating from my ribs. "Why'd you do that?"

"Because you should already know who I'm gonna marry."

"How would I know that?" I asked.

She tilted her head up so she could see my face. "Because I'm gonna marry you, silly boy."

The confidence in her slow southern drawl erased the pain in my ribs. Every word out of her mouth had always been the truth. And when she said she planned to marry me, I knew she meant it. And even if it didn't happen, she still believed it would.

Not wanting to crush her dreams, I bent my head and pressed my lips to the crown of her head. "Go to bed, sweet girl. I'm right here."

* * *

The dance blew. Ten minutes into it, all I wanted to do was get the hell outta there. Shyanne and Miley fought over who'd dance with me the entire time, regardless of the fact that I didn't go with either of them, opting to go with my friends instead. I spent the night hiding by the bleachers, visiting the men's room more than necessary, and paying a few of the guys to dance with the girls so I didn't have to. They probably thought I was gay or something since Shyanne and Miley were the prettiest girls in our class. But what they didn't get was I didn't care about that. I just wasn't feeling it with either of them. Did I try to force myself to feel something? Sure. But I wasn't one of those guys who'd act like I was into a girl if I wasn't.

JP, the backup QB who lived down the block, dropped me off after the dance. As soon as he pulled into my driveway just after ten thirty, I jumped out of his truck.

I loosened my navy tie and walked toward my back door, glancing over at Emery's house. Her bedroom nightlight barely lit her room. I hated that she needed that damn thing for nights she didn't stay with me.

I stopped in my tracks and turned away from the door, deciding to stop by Emery's house first. Once I reached her window, I tapped lightly, not wanting to scare her. "Emery," I whispered.

She peeked out the window, her face lighting up as she pushed up the window. She took in my white buttoned-down shirt, loosened tie, and khaki pants. "You look so nice. How was the dance?"

"Totally sucked."

She burst out laughing, covering her mouth so no one inside her house heard her.

"You got a pretty dress in your closet?" I asked.

Her entire face scrunched up. "What?"

"A dress. You got one?"

She nodded.

"Put it on and meet me by the big tree in my back yard."

"Why?"

"Stop asking questions and meet me there."

She nodded again and then disappeared inside her room.

I laughed to myself as I strolled through the darkness to the old tree behind my house. I definitely enjoyed spending time with Emery a hell of a lot more than anyone at that dance. People could be so fake. I hated knowing they smiled to your face and talked about you behind your back. I didn't have to worry about any of that nonsense with Emery.

I leaned back against the tree's rough trunk, scrolling through music on my phone. Country? Rap? Rock? I settled on a country playlist I knew she'd love and slipped my phone into my back pocket so her favorite country song filtered into the dark night.

"Hey," she said.

I twisted around.

Emery stood there in a frilly yellow dress her mama probably bought her for Easter or something. She was barefoot and I wouldn't have expected anything less from her.

"You look beautiful."

Her eyes dropped to her feet, embarrassed by my compliment. "Why'd you want me here in this stupid dress, Jordan?"

"I owe you a dance."

It took a minute, but her eyes slowly lifted to mine. They were glazed with what I hoped to God were happy tears.

I held out my hand. She stared at it for a long time before placing hers into it. I squeezed it and pulled her into me, bending as I lifted her hand and placed it on my shoulder so she could reach. "Now place your other one on this shoulder," I said, ticking my head toward it. She did, and I slipped my arms around her small waist. "Now we dance."

She looked up into my eyes. Words were unnecessary. I could see the appreciation in her small grin. And I loved that I was able to give her this moment.

"I told you I could dance," she said with a sass I only tolerated from her.

I laughed as I moved us from side to side to the slow beat of the music. "You did say that."

She rested her cheek against my chest and let me lead us in small circles under the thick tree branches that created a canopy above us. The song played through to the end as we shared what I was pretty sure was her first real dance.

"How many girls did you dance with tonight?" Emery asked.

"One."

"Was she any good?"

"Great."

She tipped her head back so she could look up at me. A jealous glint flickered in her eyes. "Who was she?"

I cocked my head, wondering what she'd do to whoever dared dance with me. "You," I finally admitted.

Her eyes rounded, surprise replacing jealousy. "You didn't dance with anyone?"

I shook my head. "The two of them were driving me crazy. I got out of there as fast as I could."

Her nose scrunched. "And you came to see me?"

"And I came to see you."

She pulled in a breath before releasing it with a smile. "Thank you for being the best friend a girl could ever ask for."

I pulled her into me and spent the next twenty minutes making sure her night was as perfect as mine turned out to be.

CHAPTER THREE

Grady - 17

Raindrops bounced off the roof as I scrolled through my phone. Emery pushed up my window and climbed inside. It was a lot easier for her now. Though she was still smaller than some of the other high school freshmen, she'd grown a few inches.

"*Emery*," I said, seeing her wet hair and drenched clothes. "You're soaked." I jumped up and grabbed a towel off the hook on the back of my bedroom door.

"I was out for a walk," she said as I handed her the towel and she wrapped it around herself.

I pulled my T-shirt over my head. "Here." I handed it to her.

"Thanks."

I sat on the bed as she walked to the corner of my room. She glanced over her shoulder at me. "Turn around."

I looked away, giving her the privacy she needed to change into my shirt. She was beginning to fill out and show signs she was indeed a female—something I was becoming painfully aware of. Especially now that my twin bed left little room for both of us, and my morning wood had become a daily occurrence. I knew I was an ass for doing it, but I peeked over. Her bare back faced me as she slipped my shirt over her head. I needed to look away, but I just couldn't tear my eyes away as she unbuttoned her shorts and shimmied out of them.

When it looked as if she was about to turn—and for fear of being caught and looking like a perv, I quickly looked away.

Once I heard her moving toward my bed, I looked at her. My shirt hung like a dress on her, and her wet hair was now twisted in a knot on top of her head. I slipped under the sheets, as if I hadn't just been checking out my best friend, and lifted the sheet for her. She climbed in and nestled in beside me. Instinctively, we both turned on our sides to accommodate our growing bodies. I slipped my arms around her, pulling her back flush against my bare chest. Her body was chilled from the rain, and I had this intrinsic need to want to warm her up. "You're freezing."

She shrugged.

"Were you out walking alone?" I asked.

"Yeah."

Oh, fuck. "Is something wrong?"

"You mean other than the usual?"

"Yeah."

"I just have some things on my mind."

I waited for her to say more, but she remained silent. I hated when she was silent. It always meant she was thinking. And thinking too much could be a dangerous thing, especially since our current status as best friends and bedmates was becoming a slippery slope to navigate.

"Is Lacy your girlfriend?" she asked.

Yup. There it was. "Lacy?"

She nodded. "I saw you with your arm around her at school today."

I sighed. "What's this really about? Because if it's me and you, you know regardless of who I date, you'll always be my favorite girl."

"So, you're dating her?"

"What? No. I just meant...I don't know what I meant."

A long silence descended on my room.

"Is *she* your favorite girl too?" Emery asked.

"It's complicated."

"I can keep up."

I laughed to myself. Things were becoming increasingly difficult now that Emery and I were both in high school together. She was in my bed nearly every damn night and I couldn't touch her in *that* way. Then I had girls at school—girls my own age—throwing themselves at me now that I'd filled out and could actually play football like the college-bound recruit I was.

But, was that what I wanted? Did I want girls who only wanted me for who I was or who I could someday be? Honestly? I had no fucking clue.

One thing I was sure about was my feelings were all over the place when it came to Emery. When it came to other girls. When it came to what I wanted. I was two weeks away from being eighteen, for Christ's sake. I shouldn't have been so torn over right and wrong.

"Have you taken her on a date yet?" Emery asked. "Because if you tell me you took her on a boat which is *my* dream date, I might need to kill you."

"No, I didn't take her out on a boat," I said.

"Have you kissed her yet?"

"*Emery*," I groaned.

"Did you use tongue?"

"That's it." I tightened my arms around her and rolled onto my back. Her back stayed pressed to my chest while her bare legs flailed above her.

"What are you doing?" she giggled.

"Trying to get you to stop talking."

She burst into full-blown hysterics which caused me to laugh. We'd done this long enough to know we needed to keep our voices low so my parents couldn't hear us.

Eventually, our laughter subsided. But I had a good hundred pounds on her, so I knew she couldn't get loose unless I relented. I did just enough for her to turn, twisting in my arms so she lay on top of me with her face mere inches from mine. This closeness was clearly natural for us. We'd shared a bed for six years.

But gone were the big awed eyes when she looked at me—like I was her very own knight in shining armor. Now her heavy-laden eyes showed want. Her unsteady breaths held need. "If you don't want to talk," she said. "Is there something else you'd rather do?"

My dick sprang to attention, pressing itself between her thighs.

Fuuuuuck.

"Why haven't you ever tried to kiss me?" she asked.

Unable to look her in the eyes, my head dropped to the side. "*Emery.*"

"I'm serious, Jordan. Aren't you the least bit curious?"

"About what?"

"What it'd be like."

I huffed, knowing I was in a no-win situation. This was my best friend. This was *Emery.*

"Well, aren't you?" she persisted.

"I know what it'd be like," I snapped.

"And what's that?"

I looked back into her blue eyes, the ones I wished didn't look so damn pretty gazing back at me. "Amazing."

She sucked in a sharp breath as her eyes widened, blindsided by my admission.

I was blindsided by it. My pulse quickened. What the hell was I thinking saying something like that?

A beat passed before she lowered her cheek to my chest and held onto me, like she was committing everything to memory. My words. The feel of me beneath her. Everything.

We lay like that for a long time, the stillness and quiet of the night encompassing us.

Should I have kissed her? Should I have kissed my *best friend*? I never seriously contemplated it before, and all I could come up with—as her sweet-smelling body lay on top of me—was I didn't want it to ruin the bond we had.

"No fighting tonight?" I said, breaking the long stretch of silence.

"I think it's the lull before the storm."

"Why do you say that?"

"I just have a feeling," she said. "It's been too quiet."

I had no idea what it was like to live the way Emery did with a stepdad who came home drunk ninety-nine percent of the time and took out his drunken anger on her mother. My parents were still as in love as the day they married—or so they told me.

Emery lifted her head and rested her chin on my chest, staring at me like she had something on her mind. "Will you kiss me, Jordan Grady?"

I narrowed my eyes. "Like, someday?"

She shook her head. "Right now."

My brows shot up. "Now?"

"Yes."

I swallowed the lump that suddenly shot to my throat. "Is that really what you want?"

Without hesitation, she nodded.

We told each other everything, so I knew the gravity of her asking me to do this. "Why would you want to waste your first kiss on me?"

She shrugged. "I've kinda been saving it...for you."

Fuck. Fuck. Fuuuuuck.

The number of guys who would've wanted to be in my shoes at that moment—on the receiving end of Emery's attention—was not lost on me. I heard the guys talking about her. Saw the looks she received when we walked into school every morning. I was starting to recognize the pit in my stomach as jealousy, but I quickly squashed it because it was Emery. *Emery.* The girl I would've done anything for. The girl I'd actually consider kissing so some other guy wouldn't be her first kiss— despite the risk of it messing up our friendship.

I was so screwed.

I was damned if I kissed my best friend, and I was damned if I rejected her.

What. The. Fuck?

Gauging Emery's reaction, I slipped my hands from where they rested on the dip above her ass slowly up her back. Her eyes never wavered from mine as my hands drifted from her back to her face, cupping her cheeks.

She pulled in a breath that caused my dick to twitch.

"Emery?" I said, keeping my voice as calm as I could. "Is this really what you want?"

"Yes," she breathed.

Shit.

Frantic thoughts whirled through my brain.

Don't do it. Don't do it.

"You can stop this whenever you want to stop," I assured her.

"I know."

"And I'm only doing this because I don't want some other guy to be your first kiss."

The realization of what I'd said sucked the spark right out of her eyes. "Is that the only reason?"

My eyes riveted between hers. What did she want me to say? What did *I* want to say? I didn't want to lead her on. I didn't want to ruin the friendship we'd built. But we were getting older. And I'd be lying if I said I wasn't having these weird feelings toward her.

"No," I admitted softly.

A soft blush colored her cheeks as her lips tipped up in the corners.

Fuck it. There was no turning back now.

I gently urged her face down to mine, stopping when our lips were no more than a breath apart. "This can't ruin us."

"It won't," she breathed.

I counted to three in my head then closed the distance between us, touching my lips to hers. An unfamiliar numbness spread through them as I took her top lip between mine and sucked on it gently.

Her hands slipped up my arms. Weird tingles erupted over my biceps. She didn't normally touch me with such feather-light caresses. Her hands drifted up to my shoulders before stopping and holding on tightly.

My mouth moved to her bottom lip, sucking on it as gently as the top. It was just as soft and I suddenly couldn't get enough.

I wanted more.

And, Emery did too.

Her hands slipped to the back of my head, her fingers tunneling into my hair as our lips parted in sync. I licked my way inside her mouth, my tongue moving against hers. Her hands froze, startled by the intrusion. But I kept at it. If she wanted a real kiss, I was going to deliver. Her hands moved again, bracing me to her and keeping me where I was. If this kiss was going to end, I'd be the one ending it.

I was suddenly very aware of her growing breasts pressing through the T-shirt and into my bare chest. Of her ass covered solely by underwear right there for the grabbing. I deepened the kiss, my tongue moving with purpose as I contemplated how far I should take it.

"Jordan?" my mother gasped.

Emery and I flew apart, both of us gasping for air as my mother stepped into my room with wide eyes, taking in the two of us—Emery now at the foot of the bed in nothing but my T-shirt and her underwear and me at the head of the bed in nothing but boxers.

In the last six years, my mother *never* walked into my room without knocking. Probably for fear of finding my hand down my pants. But it always gave Emery time to hide.

For some reason, probably to subconsciously stop things from escalating between her son and his best friend, she entered without announcement.

"Emery, I'm going to need you to head home, honey," my mother said kindly, though I knew a cussing-out was inevitable once she left.

Emery scooted off the bed with her eyes focused down on my floor and walked barefoot to my bedroom door. She glanced back at me briefly, before grabbing her wet clothes and disappearing down the hallway.

"What do you think you're doing?" my mother hissed when Emery was out of earshot.

I wrapped my arms around my knees, knowing I didn't have a damn clue what I was doing.

"She's fragile. You know it and I know it," my mother continued.

"She's tougher than she looks," I assured her.

"She's also fifteen. You're almost eighteen, Jordan."

"I know that."

"And despite the age gap, you know what else could happen. Your daddy had the talk with you."

"Please don't do this right now," I groaned.

"Do what? Give it to you straight?"

"She's my best friend. And if you must know, she's never kissed a boy before. She wanted me to be her first."

I watched as the knowledge registered. My mother was a hopeless romantic and quickly stifled a grin. And though the news hit her like Cupid's arrow, she still pegged me with her eyes. "You promise that's all it was?"

I thought for a beat longer than I probably should have, then nodded.

She inhaled a deep breath before releasing it. "From now on when she's here, I want the door open."

I nodded, knowing she meant when Emery visited during the day. She clearly had no idea of our nighttime sleeping routine.

But it didn't matter. Emery wouldn't return tonight. I just wondered what awkwardness tomorrow night would bring.

Emery

I closed Jordan's front door and stepped outside, my smile stretching a mile wide. He kissed me. Jordan Grady *finally* kissed me. And it didn't even matter why.

My body hummed as my fingers drifted over my lips. They were prickly in the most delicious way as I traced the path Jordan's lips had taken. Was that what love felt like? Because I was pretty certain, since I was eight years old, I'd loved Jordan Grady. He was the boy who saved me. The one who protected me. The one who made my darkest days bright.

I stared up at the stars speckling the sky. We country folk were privy to a magical display. And tonight, they were even more spectacular because Jordan kissed me. He actually kissed me. He'd been my first kiss. And if things went the way I hoped for, he'd be my last.

I knew how he'd always looked at me. I knew he'd only ever seen me as his best friend. But now that we were in school together, something had changed. The jealous way he glared at me when I walked by him in the hallways with different boys. The way he dropped everything and everyone to catch up with me when I walked alone. The way he tried to avoid being around girls whenever I came around.

He *had* to feel something.

But where did we go from there?

We'd kissed. That was for darn sure. But had he been truthful when he said he was only doing it first so no one else could?

I'd never been kissed by a boy before, but I was pretty confident the way he kissed me wasn't the way you kissed your best friend. How long would he have kissed me had his mom not interrupted? Would he have stopped or would it have gone farther?

I knew I was only fifteen, and I definitely wasn't the type of girl to lose my virginity to just any ole boy. I planned to wait. Until I was married. Until my future was a definite. If my mom and stepdad's relationship taught me anything, it was that I wanted only the best for me. And I was willing to wait to get it…and give it.

I nearly floated across the lawn separating our houses and approached my front porch, dropping down so I could stay outside a little while longer. I was too blissed-out to step inside to have reality slap me in the face. I wanted to enjoy the elation filling my body. I wanted to bask in the knowledge that I'd finally been kissed by a boy. A boy I would willingly give my heart to if only he'd let me.

"Emery?" my mother whispered from inside the house.

I swung around.

She stood in the doorway looking at me through the screen door. "I need you to get inside right now."

The urgency in her voice had me jumping to my feet. "What's wrong?"

"You need to get everything you want to take with you in the car in the next ten minutes."

My heart leaped to my throat. "What do you mean? Where are we going?" I hurried inside, following her as she frantically grabbed various items from around our small home and piled them on the kitchen table.

"We'll figure that out later. Right now, I need you to get anything important to you and get it in the car."

My heart began to bang. "I need to see Jordan."

She grabbed me by the arm and looked me in the eyes. "There's no time if we're getting out of here."

"But I need to see him. I need to explain."

"Emery, please don't do this to me right now. Get what you need and get in the car. If Wayne comes back, I may not have the nerve to do this again."

I ran down the hall to my room, my pulse pounding in my ears. I would grab my clothes and pictures of Jordan and me—the only things I really cared about—

and still have time to run over to see him. Yup, that's what I'd do.

I threw open my closet door and grabbed my backpack and suitcase from the floor. I pulled all my clothes out of the closet with hangers still intact and stuffed them into the suitcase. I left Jordan's shirt on and pulled on some shorts before sweeping all the framed pictures off my dresser and packed them into my backpack. I yanked open drawers and emptied the contents into both my backpack and suitcase. I scanned my room, pulling a stuffed panda off my bed. Jordan had won it for me at a carnival on my ninth birthday. It meant the world to me.

I stuffed it in my backpack and tossed it onto my back. I attempted to close my overstuffed suitcase by sitting on it, but it wouldn't close. I picked it up and carried it half open to the car. I shoved it into the backseat and dropped my backpack on top of it. I spun away from the car toward Jordan's house. I made it three steps before my mother called me.

"Emery. Hurry. I need your help."

My eyes jumped between Jordan's house and my own. With a discouraged huff, I jogged back inside. My mother had piles of things stacked on the kitchen table for me to carry out to the car. It took eight trips to get everything packed. Once I stuffed the final pile into the trunk, my mother jogged outside and slid into the driver's seat.

"Let's go," she said.

I looked to Jordan's house. His bedroom light was on. Was he waiting for me to come back?

"Get in," she yell-whispered.

And because I loved my mother for finally freeing us from the abuse we'd endured for far too long, I slipped into the passenger seat and pulled the door shut.

As soon as we'd reversed out of the driveway and the house we'd lived in for the past six years became nothing but a blur, I pulled out my phone to text Jordan.

My mother reached over and grabbed it. "No. No one can know we left yet. We need time to get out of town before he finds out."

"Jordan won't tell anyone."

"I said no."

I felt the tears well up, but I couldn't cry. I had to stay strong. But how could I in some other town without Jordan by my side?

Grady

I pulled my truck into the driveway after a grueling football game the following night. I glanced to Emery's house wondering where the hell she'd disappeared to. Since my mom broke up our make-out session, I hadn't seen or heard from her. It wasn't like her to go silent. What was worse was she'd never missed one of my games before. She always sat front and center. Was she embarrassed about my mom finding us? Embarrassed about asking me to kiss her?

I switched off my ignition and grabbed my phone from the passenger seat. Still no calls or texts from her. *This shit stopped now.* I pressed Emery's name and dialed her up. I lifted the phone to my ear. It didn't ring. An operator's voice informed me the phone was no longer in service. I checked the screen. I'd definitely called Emery. I tried texting her to come outside, but the text went undelivered.

My heartbeat quickened. What the hell was going on? I hopped out of my truck and hurried over to Emery's house. I rarely visited there. I never had a reason to since she always came to mine. But as I climbed the front steps of her rickety porch and pulled open the screen door, fear spread over me. I hadn't thought anything was seriously wrong until that moment. Had he finally laid a hand on her? Or worse?

I pounded on the door, pausing to listen for her footsteps to approach.

I'd kill him. I'd seriously kill him.

I pounded again.

Still there was no movement inside.

I jogged down the steps and rounded the house, moving to the side door and peering inside the door's windowpane.

Emery's stepdad sat slumped over at the small kitchen table surrounded by empty beer bottles.

Was he dead?

I pounded on the door, praying the guy moved. He may have been a son of a bitch, but he was the only one who'd know where Emery was. I pounded some more.

He stirred, slowly lifting his head and squinting toward the door. "What?" he growled.

"Is Emery home?" I called.

"She's gone," he slurred.

"Gone?"

"Left a note saying they ain't coming back."

My heart rattled off the wall of my chest. After years of abuse, Emery's mother finally did it. She'd left the monster. I wanted to be happy for them. But in leaving him, she took my best friend. How could I be happy about that?

I staggered off the steps and dragged myself home, dropping down onto our porch as I pulled out my phone. I needed to find her. I needed to know she was okay. I pulled up her favorite site. The one she posted pictures of the two of us with crazy faces. Only, her name didn't pop up. I tried another site. But still nothing.

My confusion quickly converted to anger.

How could she disappear without a heads up? How could she leave without saying goodbye? Is that why she felt bold enough to ask for a kiss? She knew she was leaving.

I scrubbed my face with my palms, pushing back the angry tears glazing them. Is this what I got for years of protecting her? Years of being razzed by the guys?

Emery Pruitt had walked out of my life forever. And she didn't even see fit to tell me.

CHAPTER FOUR

Grady - 18

"Hey, Mercy!" I slurred across the table where I played flip cup with a bunch of hot chicks from my high school. "Drink up, girl. You and me have some plans later."

The sexy redhead did as told and downed her beer as the other girls on her side of the table laughed and downed their own cups.

We played another round. My team lost and once I'd filled everyone's cups with the pitcher of beer, I chugged the rest of the pitcher, slamming it down and howling.

Everyone in the room cheered.

Yup. I was that guy.

I moved to the living room and dropped onto the leather sofa. I needed a breather if I was gonna make it past eleven. We'd won our championship game and the celebration had been going on since three in the afternoon. I was on the verge of passing out when Mercy dropped onto my lap and wrapped her arms around my neck. "Hi, Jordan."

"Grady," I snapped.

"Fine, *Grady*," she teased, obviously not understanding how serious I was. No one but my mama and ex-best friend called me Jordan.

My anger dissipated as she shifted purposely on my crotch. "You're lookin' hot…sitting on my lap," I slurred, knowing drunk Grady could say whatever the fuck he wanted. Hell, sober Grady could do the same. And he did.

She laughed. "Is that the only place I look hot?"

I shook my head, my eyes drifting over her tight little body. "You look hot everywhere."

She smiled, batting her eyelashes. "Can I tell you something?"

I could barely see her through my heavy eyelids. "What's that?"

"I've liked you since seventh grade."

My head shot back. "No shit?"

She nodded, her red curls bouncing all around. "You were just always with that little blonde who followed you around."

"She didn't follow me around," I snapped.

Clearly not sensing my escalating anger, she giggled. "The guys said you let her because it boosted your ego."

My stomach churned. I couldn't be sure if it was the beer sloshing around in my gut or her off-handed words about Emery. It had been four months since Emery left without a word. A call. A letter. And, despite my new I-couldn't-give-a-fuck attitude, I couldn't erase her from my brain. Even liquor and girls like Mercy hadn't helped shake the memory of my best friend. Of the hurt she inflicted by leaving. Of the fact that I'd been used for a safe place until she didn't need one anymore.

I grabbed Mercy's cheeks and pulled her mouth down to mine. The kiss was sloppy and in the middle of a living room filled with people, but I didn't give a fuck. I'd been the nice guy, and I'd been taken advantage of and screwed over. I'd never make that mistake again. I did what I wanted now. To hell with the consequences.

To hell with my reputation.

To hell with everyone.

CHAPTER FIVE

Grady - 21
Present Day

"How much did you lose?" Abbott asked as he hovered over me, spotting me while I bench-pressed two-fifty.

"Since the start of last season," I said, pushing the bar off my chest. "Seventy pounds and counting."

"Wow."

"Protein shakes and the gym, dude. That's all it takes," I said, lowering the bar again. "And lots of bedroom action."

"Your hand gives you that much of a workout?"

"Fuck off," I growled, struggling now to lift the bar.

He laughed as he steadied it for me.

It was late July and Abbott and I had just returned to campus, both of us offensive linemen who liked to get a jump on the season while waiting for the pre-season to begin.

"Thank God you got rid of that beard, dude," Abbott said, guiding the bar back onto the rack after my final rep. "I've never met someone with such bad facial hair."

I lay there breathing heavy and pissed that I'd gotten so much slack over a damn beard. "The ladies weren't complaining when it was between their legs."

"Dude, I live with you, remember? I haven't seen any girls warming your bed since Yvette and that was sophomore year."

"Worry about your own bed, Abbott," I snapped, hating that I'd let anyone know me as well as him—and my friend Sabrina. She'd be returning soon to chill with me while Crosby Parks, her pro hockey player boyfriend, was off doing pre-season training up north.

Abbott rolled his eyes. "Whatever. You wanna hit up the bar tonight?"

I shrugged. It was weird being back in the weight room without Caden or our star wide receiver Trace Forester around. They'd both been leaders on and off the field for the last three years. But now they'd both been drafted and were off playing professional ball.

Don't get me wrong. I was a good football player, most days anyway. But I was realistic. And a career in the pros just wasn't in the cards for me. I loved football, but I knew I wasn't good enough to be drafted. I'd probably end up a lawyer someday like my uncle.

"What the hell happened to you?" Coach asked as he stepped into the weight room.

Abbott and I exchanged a confused look.

Coach lifted his chin at me. "You're half the size."

"I lost some weight," I said, sitting up and wiping my face with a towel.

"You lost a *person*. Did you do it the right way?" Coach asked.

I nodded. "I started last season. The weight came off gradually at first. Then over the winter break, I amped up my gym routine and it started dropping off."

"Can you still defend your new QB?"

"Yes, sir."

"Good." He paused, and I hated when he did that because I never liked what followed. "Listen," he started up again. "He's good, but he's gonna need some help getting adjusted to how things are done around here."

"You asking me to take him under my wing?" I asked.

"Not asking, Grady."

Abbott chuckled as Coach walked out of the weight room.

"Fuck," I grumbled, hoping like hell Coach didn't expect me to pick up the leader role. I'd been anything but a leader over the last three years. A screw-up maybe. But never a leader.

"I hear he's a complete asshole," Abbott said. "Thinks he's a big shot now that he's Alabama's QB. I think Coach wants you to knock him down a few pegs."

"That's all I need," I groaned. "Some new prick coming in here like he owns the place."

"Dude. Don't you realize? *You* were that guy when you showed up freshmen year."

"Was not."

Abbott dropped his head back and howled. "Come on. You were loud, obnoxious, and a complete douche."

I thought back to my earlier days on campus. I was a loudmouth. I fucked around. I pushed people's buttons because I could, to hell with the repercussions.

"Actually, what am I saying? You're still loud, obnoxious, and a complete douche," Abbott said.

"Fuck off." I whipped my sweaty towel at his face causing him to jump away from it.

"Asshole."

"What's this new guy's name?" I asked.

"Flip Caruso."

I choked. "You've gotta be shittin' me."

"Nope."

"Even his name's got douchebag written all over it."

"Yup."

CHAPTER SIX

Grady

"That's him," Abbott said, lifting his chin at something behind me.

"Who?" I glanced over my shoulder with my beer bottle to my lips.

A six-foot jacked kid walked through the front door of the crowded bar with a ball cap low and off-centered.

I hated douches who couldn't wear their hats straight. "Flip Caruso."

A few girls trailed him in, their fascination with the new QB written all over their excited faces. The chump pointed around the bar at different guys who pointed back at him.

What the fuck?

Caden was a hell of a QB and he *never* carried himself that way. His skills on the field spoke for him, not some over-the-top antics when he entered a room so everyone would know he was there like this clown.

"You want me to introduce you?" Abbott asked.

I turned back to him with disgust creeping into my body. "Nope."

"You're gonna have to meet him sooner or later."

"Later."

Abbott shrugged.

A hand landed on my back. I stilled. I couldn't be held responsible for my actions if our first interaction ended with my fist in Flip's face.

"Can't a girl get a hello?"

My smile sprang free as I spun on my stool.

Sabrina stood there all blonde, hot, and sassy with her BFF Finlay by her side. Both their mouths dropped open as they took me in, their eyes about ready to burst from their sockets. "Holy shit," Sabrina said.

"What'd you do with Grady?" Finlay's dark waves whipped over her shoulder as she searched the bar around us.

I shrugged. "What? I lost some weight." And worked my ass off doing it.

"You look freaking *hottttt*," Sabrina said.

I laughed, wishing she would've looked at me that way over the past two years. I was still the same guy who pushed Finlay's buttons. The one who said stupid shit. The one who helped her get back together with her pro hockey player. "Same me. Freaking hot *and* amazing in the sack."

"Yup," Finlay said, rolling her eyes. "Same douchebag." Finlay used to be the team's water girl and was spending a couple days on campus with Sabrina before heading to nursing school in Florida where her boyfriend—my ex-quarterback Caden Brooks—had been drafted. Finlay didn't love me, but after two years, I could tell I was growing on her.

"Are you Grady?" a guy asked from somewhere nearby.

I twisted to my right.

The new QB stood there eyeing me.

"Who's asking?" I knew full well who the tool was.

"Flip Caruso." He stuck out his fist for me to bump. "Your new quarterback."

I stared at his fist, despising the way *'your'* quarterback sounded coming out of his mouth. This guy was gonna have to earn his position. *And* my respect.

Realizing I wasn't about to tap his fist, he dropped it and glanced to Sabrina and Finlay, his head shooting back and his features softening. "Hey girls. I don't believe we've met."

"Nope," Sabrina said. "We don't hang out with freshmen."

That's my girl.

"I may be a freshman, but I'm also the team's new quarterback," he assured her.

Sabrina hitched her thumb over her shoulder at Finlay. "Her boyfriend's Caden Brooks."

Finlay cocked her head. "Sorry if we're not impressed by some *college* quarterback."

Nice, water girl.

Flip let their disinterest roll right off him—or he was too stupid to realize they'd roasted his ass. His eyes shot back to mine, colder and douchier. "I've watched game tapes. You gonna have my back on the field?"

I lifted my bottle to my lips and chugged the rest of my beer. "Practice begins Monday. Time will tell."

"Time isn't what I'm worried about," Flip clipped. "Getting steamrolled because you can't do your job is my concern."

Had Sabrina and Finlay not been standing there, I probably would've leveled him with my fist.

Sensing my anger, Sabrina stepped in between us. "Grady's a hell of an offensive tackle. So be sure *you* don't get out there and blow it, freshman."

Flip snorted. "Right." His eyes jumped amongst us before he turned and walked off, joining some people at the bar.

"Well, he's a real ass," Finlay said.

"See, Grady?" Abbott called across the table. "He makes you look like a puppy dog."

"It's gonna be a long fucking season," I grumbled.

CHAPTER SEVEN

Grady

Coach's whistle blew and we huddled around Flip at the thirty-yard line. Everything about him made my skin crawl. The way he called plays. The way he ordered us around on the field. Sure, it was his job, but he needed to earn that spot. He needed to earn our respect.

Sweat pooled everywhere on my body. I searched out the new water boy, but couldn't find him. Finlay would've eventually shown up with a bottle, even those times she pretended she didn't hear me ask for one.

"Let's run an outside hook," Flip said, pulling my attention back to him.

We clapped our hands and jogged to our positions. I lined up, waiting for the snap. Once he called *hike*, I held off the defense from pummeling him. Even though I made all my blocks, I enjoyed watching every time someone else's block was missed and Flip went down.

So far for me, my new physique had worked in my favor. I thought my weight had worked for the position, but now I saw the added weight held me back from my full potential. I wasn't nearly as out of breath as I used to be. I also jogged now instead of lumbered.

Coach's whistle blew and we huddled up again. Flip called another play and we assembled on the line of scrimmage. On his call, I flew forward, totally misreading our defensive back's next move. I landed on the ground and ate a mouthful of grass as he moved around me.

I spit out the grass, got to my feet, and twisted around to see the defensive back on top of Flip.

Whoops.

They untangled themselves from one another. Once upright, Flip's angry eyes sought mine through the bars on his helmet. They narrowed, relaying what his words didn't.

"My bad, kid," I said.

"Kid?" he spat. "Fuck you!"

"A kid with a foul mouth," I corrected myself.

The fire in his eyes was comical. "You got a problem with me, Grady?"

"Now that you mention it. That pointing thing you do. Yeah. That bothers the hell out of me."

His disgust with me was evident. "Think you can make a fucking block?"

"A fucking block? Is that the same as a normal block?" I asked.

Some of the guys chuckled behind me.

Flip didn't like that. He flew across the space, shoving me in the chest. But like my run-in with Caden two years earlier, he didn't move me.

Though anger coursed through my veins, I grinned down at where he'd shoved me. "I've been working out."

Flip didn't like that either. He lowered his shoulder and charged at me.

"This'll be fun," I said, braced for the impact.

As soon as he hit me, I flailed back. So much for bracing for impact. He landed on top of me and everyone stepped back, letting us go at it. He punched at my padded chest but I easily shoved his ass off me and jumped to my feet. "Maybe I'll start protecting you once I respect you," I said as he got to his feet. "And right now pretty boy, you ain't earned it."

Flip glared at me.

"Stop acting like your shit don't stink and start acting like a leader. A true leader. Caden Brooks never would've pulled the shit you're pulling." I walked to the sideline, grabbed a bottle of water from the table, and squirted a stream down my throat.

The fucking nerve of that chump.

"Well done," a voice congratulated me from nearby.

I glanced to my side.

Coach wasn't looking at me as he grabbed his tablet from the bench and walked out onto the field.

Huh. So, that's what he meant about getting Flip adjusted to how things were done around here.

CHAPTER EIGHT

Grady

Though you couldn't see the speakers with all the people crowding my living room, the bass shook the mother-effing house. Football parties were the biggest and best parties on and off campus. And, since the entire student body had returned to campus, everyone wanted in. But I wasn't in charge of the door tonight. This Saturday night was about letting off steam before our first game. Once the season officially began, my drinking needed to be kept to a minimum.

It was past ten when I sought another pitcher of beer to guzzle. It wasn't normally on my new diet, but tonight was no-holds-barred. And I was fucking indulging.

I walked into the kitchen and grabbed an empty pitcher from the top of the fridge. I pushed myself to the front of the keg line because, let's be real, who was gonna stop me in my own house? I filled the pitcher and made my way through the first floor checking out the scene, including the fresh meat. I poured the beer down my throat as I walked, some of it missing my mouth and dribbling down the front of my white T-shirt. Fuck it. I pulled it over my head and draped it over my shoulder.

Some of the girls lining the hallway took me in. I wasn't used to the attention. Rewind. I always received attention, but it was normally because of my big mouth. This time girls were checking out my bare chest and the six-pack abs I now sported. "Yes, ladies. They're real.

And I'm definitely not opposed to you touching them."

Some of the younger girls giggled. It must've been their first college party. Some of the familiar faces, the ones who ordinarily would've rolled their eyes at me, were appreciating my reformed body. I swaggered my way toward the living room so they could really *admire* me. The room grew quiet as I entered. Were more people interested in my abs than I realized? I spun around. But no one paid me any attention. All eyes were on the front door. *Fuck.* Had the cops been called to break up the party?

As if in a bad dream, Flip-fucking-Caruso stepped through my front door. Some people shouted his name, and he did that pointing shit again. I took one step forward, ready to bounce his ass from the property. We may have been teammates, but it didn't make us friends.

"Be cool," Abbott said, grabbing my arm from behind and stopping me from moving forward. "He's your teammate."

"Right," I balked. "A great *flippin'* teammate."

"Grady," Abbott warned. "There're a lot of people here tonight. They should only see you guys getting along."

"Fuck everyone," my drunk ass spewed, loud enough for everyone around to turn and look at me.

"Dude. Be smart," Abbott persisted. "And put a shirt on."

I stood there stewing, watching the faces of all the girls in the room—even the guys in the room—eyeing our new quarterback with awe. What the hell was it about this guy? Why were they so impressed?

And then it happened.

The floor nearly dropped out from beneath me.

I blinked hard, trying to clear the liquor-induced haze from my eyes.

Was I dreaming?

Was I drunker than I thought?

I focused hard on the girl who walked in beside Flip.

Her blonde hair hung past her shoulders and a loose braid was twisted across the top of her head before disappearing into her waves. Her eyes, the lightest shade of blue I'd ever seen, searched the room. They stopped when they landed on mine, widening on contact.

Emery.

It was as though a large dose of electricity zapped through my body. My thoughts swirled in a hundred different directions as I stared across the room at the girl who'd disappeared from my life without a trace four years before.

My breath whooshed out of me.

She was alive.

She'd grown.

She was taller. Curvier. More beautiful.

Her entire face lit up and a huge smile spread across her lips.

It had been a long damn time since someone looked at me that way.

She didn't hesitate, rushing forward and weaving anxiously around the bodies separating us. She finally stopped in front of me. We weren't quite at eye level, so she tilted her back to look up at me with big twinkling eyes. "Hi."

I said nothing, just stepped forward and wrapped my arms around her, holding her close. I breathed in her fresh-scented shampoo. "You're real."

Her body shook with laughter.

I stepped back and stared down at her. "You're really alive." It wasn't my drunkenness talking. When her stepdad disappeared, I expected the worst. I had nightmares he somehow found them. Those dreams lasted for two fucking years.

Sadness shone in Emery's eyes. Hadn't she realized that's what I would've thought since she never contacted me? "Jordan. I—"

"Emery?"

We both turned quickly, realizing we were in the middle of a very loud and crowded room.

Flip stood there staring at Emery. "What are you doing?" he asked before draping his arm around her neck.

Vomit crept up the back of my throat. Why the hell wasn't she brushing his arm away?

"I…" she began, her eyes jumping between us.

Confusion grasped hold of my drunken brain. Then hatred stronger than anything I'd ever felt before spread through me, the white-hot searing kind that made you do irrational things.

The Emery I knew didn't hang out with assholes.

The Emery I knew didn't let guys hang all over her.

The Emery I knew…walked out of my life four years ago.

Then, as if I wasn't standing right there, Flip turned them away from me and walked toward the kitchen.

Emery glanced over her shoulder and mouthed, "Sorry."

Flip pointed left and right to people I had no clue he even knew who pointed back at him.

Oh, hell no.

Emery wasn't walking away from me again. Especially with him. I needed to talk to her. I needed her to explain what the hell happened. Where she disappeared to. And why the *fuck* she was with Flip.

I wove around the people crammed into the hallway, bumping them left and right without apology, until I reached the kitchen. Flip filled a red cup at the keg and handed it to Emery.

Hell to the no fucking way.

I stormed over and ripped the cup out of her hand. The beer inside sloshed back and forth, spilling over the sides of the cup. I pinned Flip with my eyes. "She doesn't drink, asshole," I slurred like a drunken dick.

Emery's eyes narrowed.

Why was she looking at me that way?

"*You're* drunk?" she said quietly.

And even though I knew why she was disgusted by my obvious drunkenness, she wasn't gonna drunk-shame me in my own house after *she* deserted me. After *she* showed up with that asshole. After *she*—

She turned to walk away from me.

I grabbed hold of her wrist.

She gasped as I pulled her toward the back door. "*Jordan.*"

"What the fuck, Grady?" Flip said, following us.

Abbott jumped between us, stopping Flip from moving outside. "Dude, give him a minute."

I tugged Emery out into the backyard until we were away from prying eyes. I stopped by the woods lining the yard and faced her. "Why are you with him?" I demanded, the slur in my voice noticeably worse.

"We haven't seen each other in four years," she said with hurt emanating from her eyes. "And that's the first thing you ask me?"

"Maybe if you'd called, I wouldn't have to ask. I'd already fucking know."

Her eyes widened.

"Does the truth hurt?" I slurred, wanting to shut up but incapable of stopping my lips from moving.

Emery's eyes had shown nothing but love and admiration for me since the day we met. But as we stood alone in my empty backyard, with music pounding the walls inside my house, I could see that look had disappeared. And in its place was disappointment. "I can't believe I thought about this moment every day for the last four years." Her eyes drifted over my bare chest with distaste. "What happened to you?" It wasn't a question. It was an observation. And I couldn't even blame her. I'd become a shell of the person she once knew.

Before I could make another brainless comment, she spun on her Chucks and stormed off. It took no more than five seconds for her to reach the house and disappear inside, leaving me outside alone. I hadn't felt that alone since the last time she left me.

Drunk and angry, I tunneled my fingers through my hair. "*Fuuuuuuuck!*" I yelled into the woods.

I had no idea what to say when I knew Emery had been right. That wasn't at all how our reunion should've gone.

"Grady?"

I spun around.

Sabrina stood on the deck staring out at me. "You okay?"

I knew the stubborn girl would stand there until she had an answer so there was no use lying. I shook my head.

She hurried down the steps. "What happened?"

I shook my head again, in no condition to unload my latest fuck-up on one of my only friends on campus.

"Come on," she said. "You don't look good. You're coming home with me."

I scoffed. "Don't promise a guy he's coming home with you if he's not *coming* home with you."

She shook her head. "With you this drunk, it's not even worth it."

"I'm not even worth it."

She wrapped her arm around my waist, and I willingly let her move us toward the back gate. We both knew it was smarter to avoid the inside of the house. Nothing good would come from me going back in there.

CHAPTER NINE

Grady

I rolled over, nearly slipping off the side of the bed. My arm shot out. The wall that normally lined the left side of my bed was no longer there. I struggled to open my crusty eyes. Once I did, sunlight infiltrated my vision, stinging like a mother. No wonder why the wall wasn't there. I was in Sabrina's room. I opened and closed my mouth, but I couldn't rid it of the cotton texture and stale beer taste.

"Morning, sunshine."

I looked to the floor where Sabrina lay under a blanket texting on her phone. "What are you doing down there?"

"I wasn't about to sleep with *you*."

"Why not?" I propped myself up on my elbow. "I would've made all your dreams come true."

"Then Crosby would've killed you."

I scoffed. "I'd like to see him try."

She rolled her eyes. "It's really a moot point since you could barely make it up the stairs to get up here. You weren't making anyone's dreams come true."

"That bad?"

"That bad," she assured me.

I fell back on the bed and scrubbed my hands up and down my face, trying to recall the night's events. How much *had* I drunk?

"You gonna tell me who that girl was?" Sabrina asked.

"Girl?"

"The one with the quarterback."

"Fuck!" I sprang up. "Emery."

"Who's Emery?"

Fuck, Fuck, fuck. "I've gotta find her."

Sabrina's face scrunched. "What aren't you telling me?"

I groaned as the previous night's events flooded my brain. I was such an idiot. Such a fucking idiot.

My parents and friends back home knew never to mention Emery. So it had been a long time since I'd actually talked about her. But I trusted Sabrina. And I clearly needed someone to talk to. So I talked.

I talked a lot.

I talked until Sabrina stared at me with pity in her eyes. "Don't look at me like that," I warned.

She huffed. "Forgive me for liking the vulnerable side of you."

"I'm not vulnerable," I grumbled. "I'm pissed."

She snorted. "There's the big baby I've grown to know and tolerate."

"Liar. You love me."

"Don't let Crosby hear you talking like that."

"Why? I'm already sleeping in his girl's bed."

Her eyes widened with amusement as she grabbed her pillow and chucked it at my head.

"I knew you girls loved your pillow fights."

She shook her head before grabbing her phone to make a call.

"Are you really calling him? Because I'm not looking to have to kick your boy's ass."

She rolled her eyes and lifted the phone to her ear. "Hey, Leigh, it's Sabrina. I've got a big favor to ask…Yeah," she said lowering her voice. "I've seen Grady's abs." She peeked over to see if I'd heard her.

I didn't even try hiding my shit-eating grin.

Sabrina shook her head as she continued her conversation. "I need you to find out which dorm Emery Pruitt's living in and her schedule…Yup. That's it. Thanks so much." Sabrina disconnected the call and looked to me. "Leigh works in the registrar's office. She'll check tomorrow."

I nodded, nervous to actually find Emery again. What would I say? Would she even talk to me? Better yet. Would she tell me why she was on campus?

CHAPTER TEN

Emery

I rolled over in bed, not having slept well at all the previous night. And though the blinds were closed, sunlight filtered into my dorm room. My roommate Raquel's comforter was still neatly in place. Guess she ended up staying with the guy she met at the party—*Jordan's* party.

God.

My heart tripped over itself at the sight of him. The feel of his arms wrapped around me brought on so many emotions. I almost burst into tears in the middle of the party. His hand on my wrist elicited tingles I hadn't felt since I shared his bed. But when his touch became tighter than necessary, I knew that wasn't *my* Jordan. My Jordan would never have handled me roughly like that.

I hadn't been lying when I told him I'd thought about our reunion every day since I'd left. I *had*. I longed for the day I could get into Alabama and be with him again. But it wasn't at all how I saw it play out. Jordan was angry. And drunk. The angry I could understand. I'd dropped off the face of the earth and magically reappeared four years later—at his house. I expected resistance. What I didn't expect was his drunken belligerence. He'd seen the life I lived with a drunk and violent stepdad. I never imagined he might've turned out like him.

My phone pinged. I grabbed it off the desk beside my bed and rolled onto my back to read it. It was from my friend Vanessa back home. **Did you see him yet?**

My fingers tapped away at my screen. **Yup**.

How'd it go?

Not good.

Call me!!!

I did.

Vanessa answered before it even rang. "Talk to me."

"He was drunk."

"Ugh," Vanessa said, understanding my disappointment. "Did you explain what happened?"

"It didn't really come up."

"I would've thought it was the first thing that'd come up."

"He was mad I was there with a guy."

"A guy?" she asked.

"Yeah. Remember the football player I met at orientation? He asked me to go with him. I knew it was a football party so I hoped I'd be able to see Jordan."

"So, he was jealous?"

"I don't really know. He was drunk and angry."

"Jeez. So, what now?"

"I have no idea."

"Girl, you've talked about Jordan Grady every day since I met you," she reminded me, as if I needed reminding.

"I know. But the way he looked at me was different."

"You guys haven't seen each other in four years. Give him a minute to let it soak in that you're back in his life."

"Yeah."

"You're not the same girl you were when you showed up in Arizona four years ago. He's gotta get used to that."

Was she right? Had I blindsided him? If the tables had been reversed, would I have been just as surprised?

Alabama was a huge campus, but I knew we'd be crossing paths again very soon. And this time, I needed to be ready.

Grady

"What do you mean there's no Emery Pruitt?" I asked Sabrina when I met her outside the history building the next morning.

"Leigh called. There's no Emery Pruitt enrolled here."

What the hell?

"Do you think she changed her name?" Sabrina asked. "You know, to start over once she left?"

I shrugged. "It's possible. She disappeared from social media."

"You could just ask Flip," she offered.

"And you could just fuck off."

She chuckled. "I figured you'd say that—well not exactly *that*. So, I asked Leigh to check if there were other Emerys on campus with different last names."

"And?"

Sabrina typed something into her phone. "I forwarded you the schedules for the two Emerys on campus. Let's track them down."

My brows shot up. "You're helping?"

"I seem to remember you staying in the library with me last year helping me find the truth about Crosby."

I nodded as I pulled out my phone and looked at the schedules she'd sent. "It says she could either be inside here." I hitched my thumb over my shoulder. "Or, across campus in the English building."

"I can stay here. I don't have class for another half hour."

"Thanks."

"Should I talk to her if I see her?" she asked.

I shook my head. "Just call me." I took off across campus. It was noon, so the sun's brutal rays beat down on everyone. My hike would require a shower as soon as I got home. It was *that* hot in Alabama in August.

I reached the building. Too impatient to wait outside, I threw open the front door and jogged upstairs to the third floor, searching the room numbers for 318. The room was in the corner and the narrow vertical window was my only means of seeing inside. I scanned the rows for Emery.

Nothing.

I slipped out my phone and called Sabrina as I made my way outside and across campus to meet up with her and hopefully Emery. "She wasn't there," I said into my phone.

"You heading this way?"

"Yeah. You mind waiting in case the professor dismisses the class early and we miss her?"

"Nope. I'll be here."

It took me a few minutes to cross campus. I dropped down beside Sabrina on the bench outside the building, needing a moment to catch my breath. We sat silently watching random people moving across campus in different directions.

"You have any idea what you're gonna say if it's her in there?" Sabrina asked.

I shook my head.

"Just be honest. Tell her you deserve an explanation."

I nodded, hoping our second encounter wouldn't be as awkward as our first. "But what if she's not the same girl I remember? What if she's a girl who likes hanging out with assholes like Flip Caruso?"

"Ummm—"

"Don't even say it," I warned.

"I wasn't going to."

"Sure you were."

"Okay, you're right," she laughed. "But, you have gotten better."

"Gee, thanks," I said sardonically.

She glanced down at her phone. "Classes dismiss in two minutes."

"Fuck." I jumped to my feet, unsure if I should go inside or wait where I stood. It didn't matter. The front door opened and a flurry of bodies shuffled outside.

Sabrina stood, shielding her eyes from the sun as we scanned the crowd. "I didn't get a great look at her the other night," she said. "I don't wanna miss her."

My eyes stayed on the moving bodies, jumping from left to right. That's when I spotted Emery staring down at her phone. Her eyes lifted from her phone and flashed around at the nearby buildings. She seemed so small on the huge campus. Just like she had the first time we'd met. Always on the verge of being swallowed up by the cruel world around her.

I didn't hesitate, jogging over to her. "Emery."

Surprise filled her face before she steeled her features, looking upon me indifferently. "Nice to see you sober."

Ignoring the dig, I smiled. "Nice to see you too."

She began to walk away, so I followed her, keeping pace with her steps. "Need help finding your way?"

She held up her phone. A campus map filled the screen.

"I'm definitely better than a map. You're heading to calculus." I pointed to the old stone building a few yards away from us. "It's that one."

"How do you know where I'm going?" she asked, moving toward the building.

I kept pace with her. "I know you," I said, playing it cool and omitting the fact I was currently stalking her. "You should know that."

We stopped in front of the building and before I could say anything, she began to climb the steps.

"That's it?"

She stopped and turned toward me. "What?"

I stared at her, unsure what I expected from someone who had no trouble forgetting about me over the past four years.

Her eyes jumped between me and the building. "I'm gonna be late."

I stared at her, wondering why she was so anxious to get away from me. I wasn't the one who left. I wasn't the one who went silent. I wasn't the one who deserved the cold shoulder.

Her patience reached its max. "See ya." She turned away again.

"Will I?"

She stopped and glanced back at me.

"Will I see you or will you be too busy with Flip?"

With disappointment in her eyes, she shook her head and turned away, disappearing inside the building.

Stupid. Stupid. Stupid.

What was wrong with me?

Why couldn't I act normal for more than a couple seconds at a time when it came to her?

* * *

I stormed into the locker room, pissed at myself for being such an asshole to Emery. *Again.* I dropped my bag in front of my locker and rummaged through it for my shower supplies. I needed to cool off before practice began.

"What the fuck did you do to Emery?" Flip's voice carried over my shoulder.

I spun around as he stalked toward me, ready to throw down again.

When was this guy gonna learn?

I stepped toward him, in no mood for his shit. "Stay out of it, punk."

"Punk?" He stepped up to me, his face inches from mine. "Can't find your own girl so you go after mine? Is that your game?"

"If you two are so tight," I said, not backing down. "Why don't you ask her about us."

"I did. She said you're nobody."

A knot twisted in my gut at his words. Had she really said that or was he just trying to piss me off? It didn't matter. I shoved him. He lost his footing and slammed into the lockers behind him.

"What the hell's going on?" Coach said, rushing into the locker room.

I pulled my eyes from Flip and glanced to Coach. "Nothing, Coach. Just making the young kids feel welcome." I patted Flip's chest to drive my point home, when what I really wanted to do was level him with a right hook.

Coach wasn't stupid. He didn't buy my explanation for even a second. But before he could ream me out in front of the others, I turned and grabbed my gear, opting to suit up away from everyone after my shower. That way I could pull it together then head out to the field with no one realizing he'd rattled me.

I purposely missed more than one block during our two-hour practice. I could take Coach yelling at me. What I couldn't take was letting Flip-fucking-Caruso win.

CHAPTER ELEVEN

Grady

I hurried into the psych building the following day, searching for room 328. I found it halfway down the third-floor hallway and peeked in the vertical window in the closed door. The door handle rattled and the door pushed open, causing me to shuffle back. "Can I help you?" the professor asked, her eyes quickly widening. "Mr. Grady? One semester of Human Sexuality wasn't enough for you? You came back for seconds?"

Professor Reyes. Fuck.

All eyes in the classroom shifted to me standing in the doorway. I lifted my hand to them, spotting Emery, wide-eyed in the last seat of the last row. "What's up everyone?"

Most of them laughed. Emery looked terrified I'd do something to embarrass her.

I looked to the professor. Same salt-and-pepper bun. Same she's-definitely-a-dominatrix-in-her-other-life glint in her eyes.

"Come in," Professor Reyes said, holding out her hand to the table in the front of the room where she stowed books and folders.

"I can wait outside."

"Sit down, Mr. Grady," she directed.

"In front of the class?" I asked, knowing there was no way I was getting out of it.

"If I remember correctly, you love being the center of attention."

I couldn't argue with that.

I walked inside and dropped down on the table, looking regrettably to Emery.

"So, we were about to get into a little game of true or false," Professor Reyes said, pacing the front of the room slow and purposefully. "You remember this game, don't you, Mr. Grady?"

I nodded, wishing I'd paid more attention to her lectures than the brunette who sat beside me last semester. I also wished I hadn't passed the class solely because Reyes wanted my ass out of her hair.

She picked up a stack of cards from her desk. "Since it's the first week of school, and I never like to put anyone on the spot, you're the perfect person for this job." She glanced down at her first card before pinning me with her eyes. "True or false? According to John Baldwin, sexuality specialist at the University of California Santa Barbara, women want multiple orgasms."

The class burst out laughing. I glanced to Emery who covered her mouth, holding back her own laughter

"Quiet everyone," Professor Reyes waved her cards at them. "Let him think."

"Nothing to think about. Obviously, they do," I said confidently.

"So, you're saying true?" she clarified.

"True."

"False. Women in their early twenties are satisfied with only one, and are usually incapable of more than one due to both their partner and their own lack of knowledge of each other's bodies."

"I don't believe it," I said.

"Am I hurting your ego, Mr. Grady? Because I hate to break it to you, but girls know how to fake it."

The girls in the class, including Emery, broke into laughter, while the guys seemed to be considering the notion.

"True or false?" Professor Reyes continued, seeming to like making me look like a fool. "The 'pull out method' works."

"Hasn't failed me yet," I said with a smug grin.

The class burst into laughter again, as Professor Reyes cocked her head at me. "Do you need a refresher on STDs, Mr. Grady?"

"Haven't gotten one of those either."

She shook her head. "So, are you going with true or false?"

"True," I said.

"False. Though it's not as bad as no contraceptive, there's a high risk of getting a woman pregnant given that sperm is released in the vagina before orgasm." Professor Reyes forged on as if she had something to prove—some personal vendetta against me. "True or false? Penis size matters?"

The class broke into hysterics, some laughing so hard they cried.

I looked to Emery who rolled her eyes. I shrugged, hoping she knew it was my apology for showing up to her class. "True," I said to Professor Reyes, knowing I had that one in the bag.

"False," she said, almost beaming at my lack of knowledge. "According to John Baldwin, if given the choice, most women would opt for a smaller penis. They're less likely to experience painful intercourse."

I sat silently wondering how the hell I was getting outta there.

"I guess it's a good thing you showed up today, given that you clearly didn't learn a single thing in my course last semester." She dropped the cards to her side and look curiously at me. "Why *are* you here, Mr. Grady?"

I hopped down from the table. "I was just looking for someone." I made my way to the door and looked back at the rows of students. "Pay attention. Professor Reyes clearly knows what she's talking about." I locked eyes with Emery and winked. Then I glanced to Professor Reyes. "But I still think you should poll the girls about that size thing."

Amused, Professor Reyes shook her head as I turned and stepped out into the hallway.

A few minutes passed before doors began opening and students filed into the hallway. Reyes' was the last to release her class. Students stepped through the door and passed by me, leaned up against the opposite wall. The guys laughed when they spotted me. Many of the girls averted their gazes. The others…well, they looked me up and down appreciatively.

"Well, that was fun," Emery said, stepping through the door and spotting me standing there.

"What?" My eyes drifted over her white T-shirt and long tan legs covered only by a torn-up pair of cutoffs. "That in there? That was Reyes showing how much she loves me."

Emery rolled her eyes. "What are you really doing here?"

"Just stalking you."

Her gaze lowered as she stifled a smile.

It took everything in me not to wrap my arms around her and pull her into a hug. But her not running away from me this time helped me resist the urge. "Can't blame a guy for missing his best friend."

Every part of her body stilled as her eyes lifted to mine. It might've been the glare of the overhead fluorescent lights, but I could've sworn tears dampened her eyes.

"Let's get out of here before Reyes spots you with me," I said. "Wouldn't want her to hold it against you."

"I thought she loves you?"

"Love. Hate. Fine line."

She snickered as we began walking down the hallway.

"Now, we can pretend I don't already know you have an hour break between classes when I ask you to grab a coffee with me," I said. "*Or*, you can make it difficult and make up some lame-ass excuse not to."

"Why?"

"Because I think we've got some catching up to do. Don't you?"

"What if I'm already meeting someone?" she challenged.

"Then you'll cancel because you just ran into an old friend who wants to know what you've been up to."

She pressed her lips together. I could almost see the indecision whirling through her brain.

I bent my neck and tried to meet her eyes. "Is that a yes?"

"Yes, you exhausting boy," she huffed. "I'll get coffee with you."

"Let's get something straight," I said, pulling the strap of her messenger bag over her head so I could carry it like I did when we were younger. "There ain't nothing boy about me. I'm one hundred percent pure Alabama man."

"Ugh. I can see the cheesiness is still alive and well."

I laughed as I turned in the direction of the campus coffee house and strolled toward it with Emery by my side. Her strides were longer than before. I didn't need to slow down for her to keep up like when we were younger.

We walked in silence across campus, me racking my brain for something interesting to say, but coming up short. Four years had passed—a long time when they were such pivotal years in both our lives. There were so many questions I had for her, but was it better for us to start fresh or rehash our past in order for us to put it behind us?

I had no fucking clue.

Soft jazz music and the scent of vanilla and hazelnut welcomed us into the coffee house. We stepped up to the counter, and the barista I knew from parties at my house greeted us, her eyes curiously jumping between Emery and me. "Hey, Grady, what can I get ya?"

"I'll have an iced coffee." I looked to Emery. "Do you still like frozen hot chocolate?"

She shook her head. "I got sick after drinking one." She looked to the barista. "I'll just have an iced coffee with extra cream and sugar."

I hated that I didn't know that. Hated that there was so much I didn't know about her anymore.

"Eight dollars and sixty-eight cents," the barista said.

I handed over a ten. "Keep the change."

"Still a big spender, I see," Emery teased.

"Only the best for you."

"Well, thanks."

I waited for our order while Emery found a table in the corner. I picked up our drinks and joined her. "So, Emery Larson…" I said, placing her drink down before sitting across from her.

She nodded. "It was important for me to keep my first name. I've always loved that it was different, but not so different that there weren't others with it."

"Only two on this campus," I assured her.

She smirked, well aware I'd been stalking her.

"And your last name?" I asked.

She pulled her drink closer and sipped out of the straw. "No one can know about my past, Jordan. We still worry he'll find us."

I nodded, understanding her circumstances. "He moved away not long after you did."

"We heard. We were so scared he'd found us but instead he went off the grid."

"I'm happy you got away from him."

She nodded. "It was so hard to leave." Something I couldn't quite read shone in her eyes before they lowered to the table. "I lost so much more than just my identity when we left."

There was no reason for her to say it. We both knew the truth. She'd lost me when she left. She'd lost the protection I provided. She lost the friend I'd always been to her.

"My mother wouldn't let me contact you." Her eyes lifted, gauging my reaction to her words.

"You were never someone to listen to your mother," I countered.

"She left him for *me*. I had to do it for her." The pain in her eyes, four years later, conveyed the depth of her situation. "She worried he was monitoring your social media and texts. You know, to find us."

I'd never considered that. I let that knowledge set in. Her stepdad had been tech-savvy. Had she contacted me via phone or Internet, chances were he would've traced the contact point. He would've found them because of me. "I worried something happened to you."

Regret blanketed her features. "I knew you would. I tried to think of ways to contact you. But in the end, I knew I'd be the reason he found us. And all my mother gave up for me would've been for nothing *because* of me."

"Where'd you go?"

"Arizona."

"So, why are you here now?"

Her eyes recaptured that spark I once knew so well. "We used to talk about me coming here to watch you play. Remember?"

I nodded.

She shrugged. "Well, here I am."

My head shot back. Had she really come to Alabama because she told me she would? Why not find me as soon as she got to campus then? Why show up at my house with Flip? I wanted to ask. Man, did I want to ask. But she was being so open. I didn't want to say anything to piss her off. "What are you majoring in?" Yup. Totally lame question.

"Social work or counseling," she said, her voice and features becoming animated. It was clear it was important to her. "I ultimately want to open a safe place for women to escape bad situations and get back on their feet, like my mom and I needed when we moved."

"Like a shelter?"

She nodded.

Of all the scenarios I played out in my head after she left, imagining Emery and her mom in a shelter wasn't one of them. "You opening a safe place for women sounds like an amazing idea. I'm really proud of you."

She shrugged, seemingly embarrassed by my praise. "I haven't done it yet."

"You will."

She suppressed a smile, but I knew she appreciated my vote of confidence. She always had. "I was able to get your games online," she said, changing the subject. "You looked great out there."

"You've been watching?"

She nodded. "I told you I would. I wished I'd been able to be at the stadium. I did make it once."

My head flinched back. "You did?"

"In Texas last year. I took a road trip with my friends. I could've sworn you sensed I was there. Your eyes scanned the seats so many times. It was as if you knew I was there rooting you on."

I thought back to that game. One hundred thousand spectators packed the massive stadium. Never in a million years had I thought Emery was there. "Thanks for making the trip. I wish you would've hung around to see me."

"It would've been too hard to see you only to take off again without being able to contact you."

Though it sucked, I understood her dilemma. Her life changed when her mom left Wayne. And though it improved in so many ways, it also required her to consider her every move. "Is it safe for you here?"

"It's been four years since we've seen Wayne. With almost forty thousand students here and a new name, I think I'll be safe. I just need to be aware of my surroundings and stay off social media. Those are a couple things you learn early on when you're starting over."

We drank our drinks in silence for a few minutes. She'd cleared so much up for me. But I'd be lying if I said I didn't need time to process it all. But I hated silence—almost as much as I hated Flip. "What's the deal with you and the idiot?" Yup. I thought I could hold off, but the thought was slowly eating away at my sanity.

"Be nice, Jordan. It's hard coming to such a big campus and not knowing anyone. He was the first person I met at orientation. And we ended up living on the same floor."

"You knew me. I'm right here."

"The campus is huge. And I didn't know how to find you."

I cocked my head. "How hard could it be to ask around, especially since your new buddy's on my team?"

She spun her cup slowly on the table, avoiding my gaze. "I'd only been on campus a day when Flip asked me to go to the party. I didn't even know it was your house."

"Stop making excuses and tell me the truth."

She pulled in a deep breath. "I didn't know how you'd react to seeing me."

Seeing the vulnerability in her eyes tugged at something inside me. Something I'd pushed down deep. "Em, don't be crazy. You were my best friend."

Her eyes cast down, and I couldn't help but hate that I'd been so tough on her at my party. It took guts for her to show up there, and then all I could do was accuse her of leaving me.

"You know Flip wants you," I said.

She nodded regrettably. "I reckon he'd like to be more than just friends."

"Damn straight he does. Watch him. I don't trust him. Anyone who enters a room and points to everyone is a tool."

She rolled her eyes. "I hate when he does that."

"Then tell him to knock it off. He's giving guys everywhere a bad name."

She laughed.

It had been so long since I'd heard the sweet sound of her laughter. I reached across the table and placed my hands over hers around her coffee cup. "I've missed you."

Her eyes dropped to my hands over hers. "I've missed you too."

And I may have been a pussy for admitting this, but my heart felt like one of the broken pieces—the ones created when she disappeared—had fixed itself back into place.

"So, where do we go from here?" she asked.

"Well, I wouldn't mind you sleeping in my bed again."

She snorted. "Jordan Grady. A gentleman does not proposition a lady like that."

My head twisted around. "You see a lady around here?"

"You're still the same stupid boy, aren't you?"

"I guess I am."

She slipped her hands from under mine and checked the time on her phone. "I should get going."

"Let me walk you."

She laughed. "Don't you have your own classes?"

I shrugged as I stood. "There are plenty of girls willing to share their notes with me."

Her smile faltered for all of two seconds before she grabbed her bag from the floor and stood. "Some things will never change," she mumbled.

Emery

"You haven't told me where you're living," Jordan said as he walked me along the sidewalk to my next class.

"Maybe I don't want you to know," I countered.

"Scared?" He laughed, and when he laughed all deep and gravelly like that, it shot straight to my toes. And, all the feelings I'd once had for him—scratch that—I *still* had for him, barreled back with a vengeance. And though my feelings remained just as strong as they'd been the night he kissed me, I needed to know if he'd ever see me as more. Being on campus was the only way to know once and for all if his feelings for me could move past the friend-zone.

"Fine. I'll have to keep stalking you," he said. "I'm harmless, you know. Except when I see you with Flip. Then I want to crush the idiot."

My brows shot up. "Jealous?"

He shrugged, his eyes averting mine. Was there a possibility he could be jealous?

"Like I said," I continued. "Flip and I are friends."

Jordan grunted. "Well, if he touches you in a way you don't like, you need to tell me."

"Agreed." I turned and glanced to the building beside us. "This is me."

He nodded.

"Thanks for the coffee. It was nice catching up." I turned to walk inside, wishing more than anything he'd stop me and tell me to stop hanging out with Flip. That he'd show me *something* that would affirm all my efforts to get there were worth it.

"Emery," he called.

My breath caught in my throat as I stopped and glanced over my shoulder. He looked even more gorgeous than I remembered with his jeans hanging low on his hips and the short sleeves of his T-shirt clinging to his biceps. "You coming to the game Saturday?"

"Wouldn't miss it."

He smiled. "Want me to leave you a front-row ticket, like the old days?"

I stilled, preparing for his reaction. "Flip already got me and my roommate tickets."

Anger flashed in his expression for a split-second and then he recovered. "I guess I'll see you there then." He turned and, in no rush at all, walked away, greeting people he knew along the way with fist bumps. But he didn't turn back.

Why didn't he turn back?

The Jordan I knew always turned back one last time to be sure I was okay. Maybe that was the sign I needed to know his feelings for me would never change.

CHAPTER TWELVE

Emery

The electricity in the stadium overwhelmed me as I stood in the front row beside my roommate, Raquel. She was excited to be at her first football game, mostly because she'd hooked up with the kicker.

The team was warming up on the field and I spotted Flip playing catch with his backup. He looked like a star out there, all tall and built with a missile for an arm. I knew this was a dream come true for him. And regardless of what others may have thought of him, he was thrilled to be the quarterback for one of the best universities in the country.

Jordan stood on the sideline, his eyes scanning the crowd behind him. When his eyes caught mine, a smile spread across his lips. He'd yet to put on his helmet so his light eyes twinkled in the early afternoon sunlight. He held his hands out to his sides as if to say this was a long time coming. I smiled back and nodded my agreement. He shook his head, seemingly amused by the way we could still read each other's minds.

Raquel leaned over. "He's hot."

"He's the first boy I ever kissed."

"No way," she said.

I gave her a sidelong glance. "Yup. And then I moved away."

"Nothing else happened between you?" she asked, her eyebrows bouncing in question.

I shook my head. "I was only fifteen. And he was older and my best friend."

"Wow. I wish I had a best friend who looked like him."

I laughed. "It definitely wasn't easy. Especially when I had to see him with other girls."

"Sounds like Flip has some competition."

I scoffed. "I don't think Jordan will ever see me as anything but the friend who left town and never called him."

"Why didn't you call?"

Oops. Too much information. I shrugged, playing it off nonchalantly. "It was easier that way."

"Does that mean he's fair game?" Raquel asked.

My stomach twisted at the thought of him with someone else. "I thought you were into the kicker?"

She shrugged. "Just keeping my options open."

I turned back to the field, saying nothing because I didn't know what to say. Could I stake claim on him when he saw me solely as a friend?

Before long, both teams lined up on the sidelines. An announcer asked everyone in the stadium to stand for the National Anthem. Just like in Texas, it was still so crazy to see Jordan on this big stage making his dream a reality in person. He told me he'd do it when he was eleven, and he actually did it. I wondered what it felt like to make a dream a reality. I gathered it was quite similar to the moment Jordan finally kissed me. I'd dreamt about that moment for as long as I could remember and once it happened, it was surreal.

The game began and the stadium erupted. Our opponents lost yardage and turned the ball back over to us in three downs. If I thought it had been loud before, that was nothing compared to the energy that ensued once we gained possession of the ball.

Our offense huddled around Flip. They clapped in unison before taking their positions. Jordan lined up to Flip's right. Flip called out something up and down his line before taking the snap. He reeled back with the ball in his hands, his eyes scanning the field for his wide receivers. A player from the other team steamrolled through the offensive line coming for Flip.

Jordan kept one hand on the player he blocked and reached over and pressed his other hand into the steamroller's chest, holding him back. Flip made a nice spiral pass down the right sideline that hung in the air. Every breath was held as the receiver, tailed by the defense, reached up with one hand and nabbed the ball over his defender's head. He was pummeled as soon as his feet hit the ground, but he'd gained thirty yards. The stadium went wild.

Ten yards at a time, Flip moved the ball down the field, with Jordan blocking for him like his life depended on it. On the seven-yard line, Flip called out a play without a huddle. On the snap, the running back crossed behind him for a handoff and took off running. Jordan ran in front of him knocking everyone in his path out of the way.

The running back dove into the end zone to score the touchdown. The stadium roared. The concrete beneath our feet rumbled as he jumped up with the ball clasped in his hand and ran toward Jordan, leaping into his arms in celebration.

The rest of the players on the field joined Jordan and his running back to celebrate the moment. Once they disengaged and ran to the sideline, Jordan's eyes searched the crowd. It's what he always did when we were kids. He looked for confirmation that he'd done well out there.

Butterflies swarmed my belly as his eyes found me standing amongst the crowd. He smiled. And the same sense of satisfaction I felt back when we were younger, back when I was the envy of so many girls, flooded my body. I returned his smile and once I did, Jordan turned away, grabbed a water bottle, and joined some teammates on the bench.

I searched for Flip. He pointed to the crowd. His eyes never found me. But then again, why would they? We were just friends. He had an entire cheering section of family and friends from back home in Oklahoma around us cheering him on.

Flip sealed our fate in the last quarter with a quarterback sneak that had him following Jordan into the end zone, leading us to a twenty-one to seven victory over Arkansas.

As the fans filed out of the stadium after the game, my feet remained in place.

Raquel followed our row out to the aisle. She glanced back, finding me still in the same spot. "You coming?" she called.

I shook my head. "I need a few minutes."

"Want me to wait?"

"Nah, you go ahead. I'll meet you at the room."

She nodded before making her way up the stairs and out of our section.

I looked back out at the field. Television cameras and a sideline reporter waited on the sideline to interview players. Flip stopped, waiting for the reporter to approach him. She didn't. She hurried over to the real star of the game. The player who made it possible for Flip to make all his passes and score his final touchdown. Jordan Grady.

I watched Jordan remove his helmet so he could speak into the reporter's microphone. His smile was so damn big and his cheeks were flushed as he answered her questions. This was his moment and everyone knew it. Flip only looked good because of him.

Something had changed in Jordan. I'd watched his first three seasons, and today was the first time I could tell he was determined to shine. It was obvious in every play. And now, that determination was there in the look in his eyes as he answered the reporter's questions.

Once the camera switched off and the reporter lowered the microphone, she thanked Jordan and turned to Flip, holding the microphone up to him.

Jordan moved away from them and his eyes found me once again, one of the few people still in the seats. He smiled and jogged over, stopping in front of me down on the sideline.

I mirrored his smile. "Awesome game."

"Obviously."

I rolled my eyes. "Flip might not realize you're the reason he looked so good today, but that reporter and the majority of the stadium knew."

He shrugged coyly and a glimpse of the old Jordan appeared.

"Oh, now you're gonna get all humble?"

He laughed.

"I'm serious. You looked amazing out there."

"Thanks to my good luck charm."

I laughed when I realized he was referring to me. "Oh, no pressure or anything."

"All you've gotta do is show up at my games."

Though I already knew I'd be there, my lips twisted in contemplation. "I may need some persuading."

"Oh, yeah?" His voice dropped to a lower tenor. "Because I can be very persuasive."

Another swarm of butterflies filled my belly. I wasn't used to him flirting with me, and I tried to stop the thoughts whirling through my brain telling me his feelings may have changed.

"Emery?"

Both Jordan and my eyes shot to Flip standing behind him down on the field. How had I not seen Flip approach? I guess, just like when I was a kid, when Jordan was around, the rest of the world ceased to exist.

"Thanks for waiting for me," Flip said to me.

Jordan exaggerated a cough.

Flip looked to him.

"You played a great game," I said, trying to redirect Flip's attention.

"Thanks to me," Jordan choked out under his breath.

Flip ignored Jordan. "Our floor's gonna celebrate tonight. You in?"

My eyes jockeyed between Jordan looking about ready to say something insulting, and Flip awaiting my response. "Yeah. Sure," I said.

"Great." Flip looked to Jordan. "You heading to the locker room, Grady?"

"Nope," Jordan said.

Anger filled Flip's face, but he pulled it together long enough to peg both Jordan and me with his eyes. When neither of us budged, he turned and walked to the tunnel, begrudgingly leaving us alone.

"You didn't ask where you guys are celebrating," Jordan said.

I cocked my head. "You're seriously gonna go all protective big brother on me now?"

"Someone's got to."

"I'm a big girl," I said. "Or haven't you noticed?"

His eyes drifted up my bare legs, over my cutoffs to the Alabama T-shirt hanging off my shoulder. "No, I've noticed."

I swallowed down my surprise and struggled to look him in the eye. "I should probably get going."

He nodded. "It was nice of you to come…see Flip."

"You know that's not the only reason I was here."

He shrugged, as if unconvinced. "See ya later, Em." He turned and made his way toward the tunnel.

I dropped down into my seat with my heart rattling around inside my chest. Was it always going to hurt so damn much every time Jordan Grady walked away from me?

Grady

I gathered up my shit after a nice long shower and took off toward the locker room exit.

"Grady," Coach called.

"Fuck," I grumbled as I turned around and trudged back toward his office.

He didn't bother to look up from the tablet he tapped away at on his desk as I stopped in his doorway. "Sit."

I dropped into the chair opposite him.

He glanced up. "How'd today feel?"

"What do you mean?"

"I mean, your game?"

I shrugged.

"Don't bullshit me," he said. "You know you played well. Probably the best I've seen you play."

"I made some nice plays."

He shook his head. I couldn't tell if he was pissed or amused. "Listen. I wasn't gonna say anything because, frankly, you aren't the most…focused player on the team. But people have been asking about you."

"What kind of people?"

"People who might be interested in taking a closer look at you."

I flinched. "Seriously?"

"This doesn't have to be the end of your football career," Coach said.

I cocked my head. "You're serious."

"Teams need a guy like you." Coach shook his head, almost amused. "I never thought those words would ever leave my lips. But, you might just have what it takes to be a leader. And, teams have begun to take notice."

"Jesus Christ," I mumbled.

"Have you considered what comes next for you?"

I half shrugged. "I just figured I'd try law school. If any of 'em will even take me."

He scoffed. "Maybe you should reconsider. See how the season plays out."

I sat speechless, never in a million years thinking any teams would be interested in me. I wasn't a marquee player. Hell, I wasn't even that likable. But maybe I actually had a chance of making it to the pros—if I didn't fuck it up.

But one thing was for sure. I needed to have a killer season. And even that wouldn't be enough. I'd still need to prepare for the pro scouting combine so teams could assess my abilities.

Making it to the pros wouldn't be easy.

But then again, nothing worth having ever was.

CHAPTER THIRTEEN

Grady

I dropped my bag down by the door as soon as I stepped inside my house. I grabbed a beer from the fridge and walked into the living room, still kind of floating on cloud nine now that Coach had sent my future goals on their head—in a good way.

Abbott played a video game on the sofa. He glanced up. "What up?"

"You up for going out?"

"Dude. I'm always up for going out. Will there be girls?"

"Unless we're going to a monastery, yeah, there'll be girls. Let's hit up the bar. If it's lame, we can crash a party."

He tossed down his controller and hopped off the sofa. "I'll be ready in twenty."

"Twenty minutes? Are you a girl?"

"I just wanna shave the areas I'm hoping a lady will be seeing tonight."

"Yup. Totally sound like a girl."

He cackled as he disappeared upstairs.

I dropped down onto the sofa and scrolled through the newsfeed on my phone. Lots of fans had posted shots of our game, mostly selfies of themselves and not me or the guys on the field. I scrolled more, stumbling upon some posts from Thursday night's preseason pro games I hadn't seen. My old teammates were dominating.

Caden Brooks had a stellar preseason game, throwing for three-hundred passing yards. I knew he would. The guy was a natural quarterback. I scrolled some more. Trace Forester had kicked some ass too. His pretty face was plastered all over the feed, having scored a touchdown in his first preseason game like the superstar he was.

Could that be my story in a year's time? I'd only ever dreamt about playing college football, telling myself a career in the pros was a pipe dream. Telling myself my football career would end after college. But now, the pros could actually be a possibility and within reach. I thought I'd been prepared for my career to end at the close of the season, but after today's game, and my part in getting us the win, I couldn't imagine not being out on a football field ever again.

Abbott only took fifteen minutes to manicure his goods, and we hopped in the waiting car. Our win was cause for celebration, as was the latest news about my future—which I planned to keep to myself so not to jinx it.

Cheers and raised glasses greeted us as we entered the crowded bar. I'd never been on the receiving end of praise when *I* entered a room like Caden and Forester had, so the reaction definitely inflated my already good mood. I did, however, refrain from pointing at everybody like the douchebag.

Before I knew it, a drink was shoved in my hand and I was ushered to the dance floor where a group of girls danced around me. I raised my hands above my head and shook what my mama gave me with the bass pounding in tandem with my pulse. The multicolor lights flashed across the faces of everyone on the dance floor as I scanned the crowd. A honey of a girl ground her ass up against me. I dropped my hands to her hips and let the music move us. Her friends eventually disappeared and it was just me and her for the next half hour.

By the bar, I spotted Flip with a group of people fawning all over him. Thankfully, Emery wasn't one of them. But if she wasn't hanging with Flip like she said she was, where was she? My head twisted around, searching the bar for her. It didn't take long to spot her in line for the bathroom. Her eyes were on mine. Her lips quirked when our gazes collided. I lifted my chin in acknowledgement. Her eyes dropped to the girl grinding up on me. I shrugged, knowing nothing else I did would make me look like the guy she once knew. And, at that moment, it sucked not being able to give her that guy.

Emery's gaze wandered away from mine, and I felt like the fuck up I knew I was most of the time.

"Are we gonna head back to your house?" my dance partner yelled over the music.

I glanced down at her. "Ummm."

"Or we could go back to my place," she said with a sly smile on her bright red lips.

I glanced to the line for the restroom. Emery wasn't there. I hated myself for even looking over there when this girl was willing to go home with me. This was high school all over again, and I was feeling guilty for being with other girls. There was nothing wrong with it. It was natural. But knowing I had Emery in my life always made me feel guilty. Maybe it was the fact that she used to like me. Maybe I didn't want to hurt her. But now, we were both grown. And her crush on me was clearly over. So, why did I still care?

I looked down at the girl I'd spent the last half hour dancing with. She was smiling at me. She had a cute face. A nice body. But I did what I'd always done when Emery was in my life. "Sorry. I'm not looking for this to go any further than the dance floor."

The girl's mouth opened then closed into a tight line. If ever a person were to haul off and punch me, it should have been her at that moment. But she didn't. She spun away from me, leaving me standing alone in the middle of the dance floor.

The music suddenly changed to a party anthem. The noise in the room reverberated off the walls as the whole bar jumped around and sang along to the lyrics.

Someone tapped me on my shoulder and I turned around.

Emery stood there, her eyes dancing with amusement. Her skinny jeans and sparkly black tank top made her fit in with the rest of the girls in the crowded bar. But she wasn't just any girl. "What'd you do?"

My eyes narrowed.

She ticked her head over her shoulder. "To make her ditch you in the middle of the dance floor?"

"I told her I wasn't taking her home with me."

Emery stared at me, her brows drawn. "Why not? Isn't that what you college football players do? Get girls to go home with you?"

I shrugged. "Not sure. You wanna come home with me?"

She laughed and her entire face lit up like it did when we were younger. And that right there. *That* was the reason the other girl wasn't coming home with me. She didn't look at me like Emery did.

The thought hit me hard, nearly leveling me.

I wanted to be looked at the way Emery looked at me—like she saw the real me. I deserved that.

"If that's your game," Emery said. "I can see why it's not working."

"Oh, yeah?"

She nodded. "A girl likes to feel wanted. She doesn't want games. If you don't plan on taking it past the moment, make it clear to her."

I grabbed Emery's hands.

Her eyes dropped to our linked fingers. "What are you doing?"

"Dancing with you. Though, I'd say our night under the big tree might've been more memorable."

Her head shot back. "You remember that?"

"Of course I remember that."

She swallowed down hard, my words obviously affecting her. "Flip's gonna be wondering where I am," she said. "I came with him."

"Flip!" I shouted across the dance floor toward the bar where he stood.

"What are you doing?" Emery said, ducking her head into my chest.

Flip didn't hear me, but other people got his attention for me. He turned and his eyes found me, narrowing when he spotted Emery with me.

"I'm gonna dance with Emery!" I called to him before turning us away from him.

Emery pulled her head back and looked up at me. A flicker of amusement lit her eyes. "Why'd you do that?"

"Weren't you just the one who told me not to play games? To make things clear?"

"To a *girl*."

"Flip's as feminine as they come. And by the way, he didn't say you couldn't dance with me."

She rolled her eyes. "Obviously. He's not my boyfriend. And even if he was, no one tells me what to do."

I pulled her against my chest, moving my hips playfully against hers as I held our linked hands out to our sides.

She laughed but tried to resist dancing, forcing our hands down and standing still.

I didn't give up that easily, holding her closer. And soon her resistance waned.

The song eventually turned to a slow one. Emery tried to move back which just made me drop our hands so I could wrap my arms around her waist. She tensed. But with our bodies that close and me showing no signs of releasing her, she had no choice but to wrap her arms around my neck and move with me.

I buried my nose in her hair. The faint scent of coconut worked its way into my senses. She hadn't worn anything scented when we were kids. Back then she smelled like whatever we'd done that day. "You were right," I said.

She lifted her head so she could see my eyes. "About what?"

"You *are* a good dancer."

Her perky little nose scrunched. "When did I say that?"

"When you told me I should take you to that high school dance with me."

"You should've." She shook her head. "I can't believe you remember so much."

I leaned into her ear. "You were the best part of my childhood, Em. Of course I remember."

"Why do you keep calling me Em?"

"Because we're starting over. My new best friend—and lucky charm—is Em."

"*Am* I your best friend?"

"I sure hope so."

"What's being your best friend entail these days?"

I smiled. "Well, for one, dancing with me when I need a dance partner."

She laughed and the sound was like hearing my favorite childhood song, familiar and filled with the best memories.

"Playing games when I need a video game partner."

"I hate video games," she said.

"Since when?"

"Since forever."

"Then why'd you play with me all the time?"

She tilted her head to the side, as if I should already know.

"How about checkers?" I continued. "Remember you used to kick my ass at checkers?"

"I could *still* kick your ass at checkers."

I chuckled. "There are gonna be times I need someone to escort me to a party."

"Sounds like you need a wingman, not a best friend."

"Not true. I don't need you helping me pick up girls."

Her brows shot up.

"That's what a wingman does," I explained.

"Well, good, because I've never been good at thinking anyone is good enough for you."

My heart stuttered in my chest. It had been a long time since someone thought I was worthy of anything good. I'd made sure of that. Pissing people off was my MO. It kept most at arm's length. But the single observation from my oldest friend reminded me of the truth. "I've missed you."

A smile tugged at her lips. "Good."

"Emery?"

Her head twisted over her shoulder.

Flip stood there, impatience evident in his eyes. "We're gonna head out. You staying?"

Her eyes cut back to me, indecision written on her face. But it took no more than a second for her hands to drop from my shoulders. She turned to Flip. "Nope. I'm coming with you guys." She glanced back at me. "Thanks for the dance."

And then she was gone, following Flip like one of his minions.

I didn't like watching her walk away. Last time had been torture. I'd never let that happen again.

Emery

I stepped inside my room after my shower and dropped down onto my bed. The night had been…unexpected. I wanted to stay with Jordan, but I'd come with Flip and my hall mates. I wasn't trying to make this a game. I'd been truthful when I told Jordan that Flip was my first friend on campus. I wouldn't ditch him now that I'd found my old friend. Even if that old friend held a huge piece of my heart.

My phone pinged on my nightstand. I grabbed it and flopped back onto my bed, finding a text from an unfamiliar number. **Just so you know. This isn't about him or me. It's about me and you.**

Who is this? I texted back.

Who do you think it is?

I stifled a grin as I typed my response. **Flip?**

I hate you.

I don't think you do.

There was a long pause before the bouncing dots started up and his response appeared. **I liked dancing with you.**

Oh, now I know who this is. Roger, right?

He fired back. **Who the hell is Roger?**

I laughed, having way too much fun at Jordan's expense.

Fine. I see how this is going. Just wanted to make sure you got home ok.

My belly rippled like it had so many times before when I'd hoped his concern for me meant something more. **I did.**

Alone?

Alone.

Night Em.

Night Jordan.

I tossed my phone down and fell back on my pillow.

I was so screwed.

CHAPTER FOURTEEN

Grady

Monday afternoon, Sabrina and I sat in the dining hall by the window overlooking the campus.

"You guys looked good out there Saturday," she said. "Even Caden said so, and we know how he feels about you."

"He said that?" I asked, trying not to sound too surprised my ex-QB checked out our game and thought we looked good.

"He told Finlay. He wanted to know what Flip's doing to get you to protect him and the guys so well."

"What'd she tell him?" I asked, before sucking down a mouthful of soda.

"You're after Flip's girl."

A spray of soda shot out of my mouth.

It would have covered Sabrina had she not moved to the right. "*Grady!*"

"Shit. Sorry." I grabbed a handful of napkins and wiped up the mess between us on the table.

"I've thoroughly lost my appetite," she grumbled.

"Why'd you tell her to tell him that?"

"It's the truth, isn't it?" Sabrina asked.

I dodged her eyes. "First of all, she's not Flip's girl."

"Ah, ha! I knew it."

My eyes cut back to her.

"You totally bagged yourself," she said.

I shook my head. "I don't know what I'm feeling. She keeps turning up. And now she's all grown up…"

"And no longer off-limits?" Sabrina asked.

I dragged in a breath, considering her question. Was that what was happening? Was I confused because I no longer needed to keep our relationship platonic? Or did I just hate seeing her with Flip? "I have no idea."

"There's only one way to figure it out."

"Yeah? What's that?"

Emery

There was a knock on my door Monday night. I crawled off my bed, gladly ditching the essay I'd been typing all evening. Raquel had taken off for the showers a while ago. She probably forgot the code again. I opened the door, surprised to see Jordan standing there. He donned a ball cap pulled down low on his head, a white T-shirt stretched across his chest, and basketball shorts low on his hips. Yum.

"Hey." His lips tugged up in one corner, obviously noticing my surprised appraisal.

"How'd you know where I lived?"

"I've got connections."

"So, you use your spot on the football team to assist with your stalker tendencies?"

Amusement flashed in his eyes, and I caught yet another glimpse of the boy I once knew. Those glimpses were becoming more frequent the more time I spent with him.

I moved forward, blocking the doorway in case he tried to come in. "What are you doing here?"

He peeked over my shoulder into my room. "It dawned on me that I've never seen your room."

"Why do you need to see my room?"

"Who do we have here?" Raquel asked, stepping up behind Jordan.

He turned around. I could only imagine his delight at finding her standing there in nothing but flip-flops and a towel, her wet hair in a knot on top of her head. He moved out of the way so she could step into our room.

"Oh, you're that football player," Raquel said.

A smirk slipped across his lips. "Which football player?"

My heart drummed faster. What did she plan to say? Was she going to tell him what I'd told her about him?

"The hot one who made all those blocks so Flipster could throw the ball."

"That's me," Jordan gloated. "And I like your nickname for the fool."

She laughed.

"Sorry, Em." Jordan's eyes cut to mine. "I know he's your guy."

"He's not my guy," I said matter-of-factly.

"It does seem like he is," Raquel added as she pulled open her drawer and removed a pink thong, obviously for Jordan's benefit.

"I don't care how it seems. We're friends," I assured them.

"Woah, no need to get defensive," Jordan said, which just made me more defensive. "No one faults you if you like him."

"I don't like him," I huffed.

"You spend an awful lot of time with someone you don't like," Raquel said as she stepped into her thong and pulled it up her legs and under her towel.

Did she have no shame?

"*You* hang out with him too," I said to her before glaring at Jordan. "And why are you even here?"

"Just wanted to hang out with my best friend."

I tipped my head to the side. "Doing what?"

"We could do what we used to do." His eyes slid to my bed and his mouth pulled up in one corner.

"And what's that?" Raquel asked.

"Playing football. Swimming in the creek. You know. Kids' stuff," I explained.

"Or we could watch a movie," Jordan said, stifling a smile.

I stood there, pondering his motives. Did he really believe we could go back to being best friends that easily?

"If you won't, I will," Raquel said to me.

I glanced to her. Was she trying to help? Or would she really watch a movie with him with me right there? I looked back to Jordan. "Fine."

"Oh, shoot. I just remembered I promised to help Kate with something down the hall," Raquel said.

I suppressed a smile knowing she didn't know a Kate down the hall.

She tugged open a few drawers and grabbed some clothes, clutching them to her stomach as she moved to the door. "I'll change there." And with that she slipped out of the room, closing us off to the outside world.

Suddenly, the room felt tight. Any way I moved, Jordan was in my space. His just-showered scent quickly replaced the scent of Raquel's shampoo. And I had no idea what to do with myself. I lowered myself down onto the edge of my bed and waited for him to say something.

"Well, this is awkward."

Nervous laughter burst out of me. "No more awkward than Raquel getting dressed in front of you."

"Nothing I haven't seen before," he said.

My lips formed a tight line as I tried to ignore the hollow in my chest.

"I haven't seen *her* like that," he explained. "I just meant. You know what I meant."

I nodded, though I couldn't stop the bout of sadness from washing over me. It wasn't like I thought he'd stay a virgin forever. I just hated the thought of him in bed with anyone but me. That was our thing—the closeness I always felt in his arms. I knew it was foolish after all this time, but I wanted that reserved solely for me. I glanced down at my cutoffs and T-shirt. "Don't get any ideas. I'm not changing."

"Good. You look perfect."

I refrained from sighing because I was pretty sure he had an arsenal of lines like that for whichever girl would listen. "What do you wanna watch?"

"I'm guessing porn is outta the question?"

I rolled my eyes.

"How about a good horror movie so you need me to protect you?"

"Are you ever serious?"

"Why do I need to be serious?"

I shrugged. "It just seems like you've got an answer for everything."

"I do."

He'd changed. I guess I should've expected that to happen in four years. But it made me wonder. Was that what happened when guys grew older? Or did it have something to do with me leaving? Would he have changed had I not left?

I grabbed some throw pillows from my bed and tossed them to the floor. My stuffed panda, which had been tucked between the pillows, tumbled into view on my bed. *Shit.*

"Is that?"

I scooped it up and placed it on my desk. "Yup."

"You kept it?"

"Of course." A stretch of silence passed as I sat down on the small area rug, pushing the pillows against the side of my bed and resting my back against them. I looked up at Jordan. "You gonna sit?"

He quirked a brow. "Don't trust yourself with me on the bed, huh?"

"Why wouldn't I trust myself? We're friends."

He sat down beside me, his body pressing to my side and his scent filling each and every one of my breaths. "Just saying."

"You're actually not saying anything," I said.

He lifted his hat and turned it backward on his head. "Just saying, the last time we were in the same bed things got a little…intense."

The memory of our one and only kiss had carried me through some very dark days. And the fact that he remembered—that he remembered so many important moments—solidified for me that what we had back then had been real. It might have only been friendship, but it had meant something important to both of us. "Intense?" I dared to ask.

"What would you have called it?"

"A nice moment between friends," I said, trying to be nonchalant, though the memory was as fresh as the night it happened.

"If that's how you treat all your friends, count me in." He crept toward me, his lips pursed and aiming for mine.

I shoved him off. "*Jordan.*"

He laughed. "I'm just teasing you. Tell me you still know how to be teased."

"Of course I can be teased. I just don't know where those lips have been over the last four years." I said it jokingly, but the thought had plagued my mind for four long years.

He laughed.

"Have you had many girlfriends?" I asked nonchalantly, though my heart began to pound away in my chest as I braced for his response.

Jordan's body went rigid beside me. It was the exact opposite of the reaction I expected from him. "A couple. No one special."

"Why not?"

He shrugged. "They were good girls. Just not right for me."

I bumped him with my shoulder. "You too high maintenance or something?"

"Nah. Just not feeling it."

I nodded, his admission easing my unwarranted jealousy.

"How about you?"

"I'm not high maintenance," I teased.

This time he bumped me with *his* shoulder. "You have many boyfriends?"

I shook my head.

"Just one or two?" he persisted.

I shook my head, hoping he dropped it.

"More?"

I closed my eyes, and my embarrassment slowed the shaking of my head.

"This mime-game you've got goin' ain't working for me, Em. You've actually gotta speak."

I opened my eyes, steeled my features, and admitted my truth. "I've never had a boyfriend."

Jordan's head shot back. "But you're so hot."

My breath caught in my throat.

Noticing my surprise, he quickly amended his words. "I mean, you must've had guys lined up for you."

For as long as I lived, I'd *never* forget him calling me hot.

"No one special," I admitted. I'd dated. Gone to parties and dances. But none of those guys lived up to my feelings for Jordan.

He nodded like he understood. But did he really understand why I hadn't had a boyfriend? Why no one would ever be enough?

"I guess we've got to lower our standards," I joked. "At this rate, no one's ever gonna be right." My gaze dropped to his lips. Not for a single second had I forgotten how they tasted and felt against mine.

"What about Flip?" he asked.

"What about him?"

"*He's* not right?"

My eyes lifted to his. I hadn't forgotten how pretty they were when they were looking at me. "You know he's not."

"How would I know that?"

"Because...I—"

The door handle rattled and the door swung open. Raquel walked in. "Sorry to interrupt."

I sat back, distancing myself from Jordan's penetrating gaze. "You're not interrupting," I said to Raquel, though my heartbeat pulsed like a ticking time bomb.

I could've sworn Jordan huffed beside me.

Raquel hurried to her desk and grabbed her laptop. "Just remembered I needed this." She hurried back to the door and was gone before we could respond.

I pushed myself to my feet and walked to my own desk, needing the distance to bring me back down to the here and now. I grabbed my laptop.

"You were about to say something when your friend came in," Jordan reminded me.

I played dumb as I turned around with my laptop in my hands. "I was?"

"I thought so."

I shrugged as I sat down beside him and called up some movies to stream. I skimmed through the horror movies, thankful we'd been interrupted. My mouth was getting ahead of itself. And in no way was I ready for that type of rejection.

Jordan pointed to a movie I never would've watched alone. "I hear it's really scary."

"Oh great," I laughed.

"Don't worry. I'm right here."

I clicked on the movie and the eerie intro music filtered through the speakers and the credits flashed onto the screen.

"You sure you don't want to watch it on your bed?" he asked. "You know, get a little more comfortable."

I nodded, knowing I'd never be able to concentrate on the movie with Jordan Grady in my bed. "I'm sure."

CHAPTER FIFTEEN

Emery

"So, you're telling me nothing happened?" Raquel asked, her mouth filled with a blueberry muffin.

I sipped my iced coffee. "Nothing happened."

"But why? You two are so stinking cute together."

"We're not together." My gaze wandered around the crowded dining hall. "We never were."

"That doesn't mean things can't change."

I picked up my raisin bagel and tore off a piece. I'd always wanted Jordan. Plain and simple. So why wouldn't I let myself admit that to her? Or him for that matter? Was I that terrified of being rejected? He'd teased me about wanting to kiss me or lay in bed with me, but that didn't necessarily translate to him wanting a relationship with me.

Raquel stared at something behind me. "Speak of the devil."

I glanced over my shoulder. A group of football players filed into the dining room with Jordan leading the pack. He didn't see me as he pulled out a chair and flipped it around so he sat backward at a table with his friends. I looked back to Raquel. "How about you and the kicker?"

"Eh." She shrugged. "He's a kicker and not a QB for a reason."

"Am I supposed to understand what that means?"

"It means he's not aggressive. I had to do all the work."

"*Ohhh,*" I said, hoping that spared me the dirty details.

"Oh, what?" Jordan was suddenly there, slipping into the seat beside me.

"Hey, football player," Raquel cooed.

I was beginning to realize she wasn't flirting. It was just the way she talked to all guys. "Raquel was just talking about your kicker," I explained.

"You and Jonesy?" Jordan asked her.

"I think our time together has run its course," she explained.

"Well, let me know. There are a lot of other guys who might be more your speed."

"So, you're a matchmaker now?" I asked him.

He leaned into me and whispered into my ear. "I'm a lot of things."

The tenor of his voice sent goosebumps scampering up my arms. "Oh, yeah?"

Raquel laughed, probably hearing the fear in my voice.

Jordan grinned. "Listen, Em. I have a serious question for you."

My brows shot up.

"My mom's birthday's Wednesday. I'm heading home and thought maybe you'd like to come."

"Oh, I…" Thoughts of going back to a place I both hated and loved sent my body on edge. Was it safe? Would anyone see me? Could Wayne still be lurking around? "I probably shouldn't."

"My parents would love to see you."

"It's not that…"

"Well, what is it?"

How could I tell him I still lived in fear of my ex-stepfather? I wanted him to see me as strong and confident. "I've got class."

"Bio," Raquel said. "And I'm in the class. You can get the notes from me."

I cocked my head, needing her to have my back. She clearly didn't get the memo. But then again, why would she? I hadn't opened up to her about my past.

"Come on, Em. I'm not opposed to begging," Jordan continued.

I pulled in a breath and let all the reasons it was a bad idea flee my mind as I stared into the beautiful blue eyes I'd dreamt about for the last four years. "Fine."

Jordan smiled as he pushed his chair back and stood. "Great. I'll pick you up Wednesday morning." He didn't wait for a response, probably because he knew me. And the longer he gave me to think about it, the more apt I'd be to back out.

"He wants you," Raquel said as he made his way across the crowded room, waving to people and bumping fists.

"I'm scared to let myself believe it," I admitted.

She tilted her head, her eyes assessing me sadly. "In life, you've gotta take risks."

"Says who?"

"Says anyone who's gone after what they've wanted and gotten it."

"Easier said than done."

"Maybe. But that guy." She lifted her chin in Jordan's direction. "I'm thinking he's worth the risk."

I glanced over my shoulder at him. He was laughing with his friends. I used to be the friend he laughed with. And though I still wanted to be the one he laughed with, I knew down deep I wanted to be the one he did more with.

So much more.

CHAPTER SIXTEEN

Emery

I'd woken up late and was struggling to brush on some makeup when there was a knock on my door. *Shit.*

"Want me to get it?" Raquel asked from her bed where she hadn't bothered to get up yet, even though she promised to take notes in our class that began in two minutes.

"No, it's fine. You've got a class to get to," I reminded her.

She groaned and threw her covers over her head.

With a deep exhalation, I grabbed the doorknob and pulled open the door.

Jordan stood there with a ball cap on backward. Just looking at him sent goosebumps scrambling up my arms. "Ready?" he asked.

I glanced down at my skinny jeans and Alabama T-shirt. "I overslept and am kind of a mess."

"You're beautiful," he said.

My eyes flew up at the same time Raquel sighed.

"Can I have you?" she asked him, her head suddenly out from under her blankets. "Unless you're already taken, of course."

He gazed at me. The look in his eyes held questions—lots of unspoken questions. "Nope. It'd take a special girl to handle this much man."

I grabbed a sweatshirt from my closet before glancing to Raquel. "Still want him?"

"I don't mind a little cheese with my muscles," she said.

I pegged her with my eyes. "Take good notes."

She rolled her eyes.

Jordan and I walked outside and toward the cars parked in front of my dorm.

I looked for his old red truck, so the souped-up black one that beeped when he pushed the button caught me off guard. "New truck?" I asked, reaching for the handle.

Jordan bumped me out of the way and opened the door for me. "My parents got it for me. They thought it'd be a lot safer than the old one. I think they thought it would get me to come home more often, too."

"You don't visit them?"

"Usually just holidays." He rounded the front of the truck and jumped inside.

"Why just holidays?" I asked as I closed my door and buckled in.

He shrugged. "I talk to them all the time."

"Have you told them about me?"

"Was I supposed to?" he asked, as he switched his truck on, the loud engine roaring to life.

I shrugged, though disappointment twisted my insides.

He laughed. "Of course I told them."

I looked to him, the twisting ceasing. "You did?"

He nodded as he pulled away from the curb.

"And?"

"They were happy to know you and your mom were all right."

I lowered my head and nodded, feeling uncomfortable with the fear I instilled in them by disappearing.

"They were happy for me too," he added as he pulled out onto the main road.

My eyes cut to his. "For you?"

"Yeah. That I got my favorite girl back."

My belly rippled at the sweet words he uttered.

He stayed focused on the road in front of us. "It was hard for me after you left."

"I'm sorry."

"Don't do that." His eyes moved between me and the road. "Don't apologize for something out of your control. It just sucked that my biggest fan was no longer at my games. My partner in crime wasn't around to hang out. And my bedmate was no longer there for me to snuggle with."

I nodded, having felt the exact same way.

"But you're back," he said, reaching across the center console and placing his hand over mine in my lap. "And I'm not losing you again."

I fought back the tears blurring my vision. He was saying everything I'd dreamt he'd say.

Jordan cleared his throat. "Now that that's been said…" He opened our windows then reached for the radio and cranked up some good ole country music.

I threw back my head and laughed as we hit the highway. The wind whooshed through the open windows and blew my hair around my head. Being with Jordan again, away from the huge college campus filled with unfamiliar faces that held no memories of us, felt so natural. So easy. Like being home. Did he feel it too? "I missed this," I shouted over to him.

He reached forward and lowered the music. "What?"

"I missed this. You and me."

"What do you think I've been trying to tell you?" he asked incredulously.

Before long, we were pulling down the same familiar roads where we'd spent our childhood. The hair on my arms stood on end as we turned onto the road and neared my old house. The new owners had fixed it up. The broken porch boards had been replaced, so had the screen door. Window boxes filled with colorful flowers sat on the top railing. It looked like such a nice warm place to live…now.

Jordan turned into his parents' driveway. The sight of *his* house flooded me with welcome nostalgia. I glanced to the window on the side of the house. Jordan's room. The night I approached that window, so sad and forlorn, I'd met the best friend a girl could ever ask for. Sometimes it felt like a lifetime ago. Sometimes it felt like just yesterday.

Sensing my range of emotions, Jordan reached over and linked our fingers. "You okay?"

I nodded.

He switched off the engine and looked to me. "You sure? I don't want you feeling uneasy."

I tilted my head to the side and stared into his concerned eyes. "You're here. I'll be fine."

His lips pulled up in the corners, and while I knew he easily could have inserted a cocky comment right there, he didn't. "Come on. Let's surprise them."

"They don't know we're coming?"

He shook his head. "They don't know *you're* coming."

I pushed open the door and hopped out, suddenly feeling even more anxious.

Jordan met me at my side and smiled down at me. "This is so crazy."

"What?"

"Having you here again."

My insides rippled something fierce. The way he looked at me. The way he made me feel. They had to equate to more than just friendship. They just had to.

"Emery?" Jordan's mother called from their open front door.

Jordan and I turned to her, not realizing she'd been standing there.

She hurried down the steps and wrapped her arms around me, holding me tightly to her. "Oh, honey. You're here," she gushed. "We're so happy you're okay." She pulled back, her hands still gripping my arms tightly so she could look at me. "Look at you. You're even more beautiful than when you left."

My face pulsed with heat.

"Mom, leave her alone. You're embarrassing her," Jordan said.

"Well, don't you think she's more beautiful?" she asked him.

I glanced to Jordan with my brows raised in question.

"She already knows I think she is," he said.

I stifled a smile as I stepped back from his mom. "Happy birthday."

"Thank you," she said. "This is such a wonderful gift."

Jordan moved to her and wrapped his arms around her, lifting her right off her feet. "Happy birthday, Mom."

She squealed with laughter.

I wished—like I always had—I was part of their family. Part of the bond they shared. I loved my mom more than anything in this world, but being part of a family—with a happy mom and dad—was what I'd always wanted. Sure, I knew a perfect life was not necessarily attainable, but I still hoped one day I'd have it.

"I hope you're hungry," Mrs. Grady said as Jordan released her.

The three of us walked inside their house. The smell of her comfort food cooking hadn't changed one bit.

Mr. Grady stood inside the kitchen, greeting Jordan with a hug. "Good to have you home, son." He released Jordan and turned to me, pulling me into a hug. "You too, Emery. We missed you."

It felt odd to be hugged by Mr. Grady. By any man, really. My stepdad never hugged me. And I never met my real dad. But as soon as Mr. Grady released me, I felt bereft. I hadn't realized how comforting it was to have people care so much about me and my well-being. Had they been sad when I left? Had they been just as angry as Jordan? Or did they realize the hell we'd been through and the urgency for us to leave?

We ate at the kitchen table, laughing—usually at Jordan's expense—and listening to Jordan's stories about everything football. His parents had been at his first game, but I hadn't seen them. I promised to sit with them next time. Mrs. Grady also told us about her first year being retired. She'd been an elementary school teacher, and Mr. Grady claimed she was bored out of her mind and in desperate need of a hobby. According to him, her latest pastime was asking him repeatedly if he washed his hands. "Old habits die hard," she claimed.

Once we'd finished lunch, she stood from the table and gathered our empty dishes. I stood to help her. "Sit down, honey. I've got them," she said.

"Nope." I grabbed a couple serving dishes. "It's your birthday and I'm here to help."

She laughed as we placed the dishes down on the counter.

Jordan and his dad talked about football, and I could tell she wanted to give them time to catch up.

"So, you and your mom have been good?" she asked, obviously treading lightly.

"Yeah. She misses me now, but she's been busy with her job." I pulled open the dishwasher and placed the dishes in as she rinsed them. "She got back into real estate. Selling houses and stuff."

"Oh, that's great. She deserves a happy ending. So do you…" She paused and looked me in the eyes. "And Jordan."

The way she added *Jordan* made me wonder if she thought we were destined to be more than friends like I always had. Or if she just wanted us both to find happiness.

Once we'd cleaned everything, Jordan stepped up behind me. My entire body stilled as the warmth and solidity of him called to every cell inside me. Without warning, he wrapped his arms around my shoulders and pulled me playfully into his chest. He had no idea how the gesture sent my body buzzing. "She done helping here?" he asked his mom.

"Yup. She's all yours." Mrs. Grady looked to me. "Thank you for helping, Emery. It's been some time since I had any help in the kitchen." She purposely pegged Jordan with her eyes.

He laughed as he released me and leaned over to his mom, kissing her cheek.

Her smile beamed at the love shown by her only son.

I followed Jordan from the kitchen down the hallway to his room. He stepped inside, but I stopped in the doorway, gazing around at the room where I'd spent most of my sleeping hours. It looked different. He'd painted the white walls blue. The pictures of the two of us at different stages he once tucked into the corner of his mirror were no longer there. Had he torn them up? Thrown them out?

My gaze wandered to his bed. He'd replaced his football-themed comforter with a plain red one, but the oak headboard was still the same. Being in his arms in that bed had been the only place I felt at ease. Untouchable. Protected.

"Whatcha thinking?" Jordan asked as he sat down on the edge of his bed.

I shook my head slightly, chasing away the thoughts. "Just remembering."

He glanced down at his bed. "It felt empty without you."

I nodded, hating the constant reminders of what I'd done to him. To us.

"Come sit." He patted the empty spot beside him. "I won't bite."

"I'm not convinced," I said as I walked over and sat beside him.

"See. No teeth."

I observed the room from the angle I used to sleep at. "Thank you for everything you did for me."

"You don't have to thank me."

I nodded. "Yes, I do."

"I'll always have your back."

I had no doubt about that.

He bumped me with his shoulder. "Guess what?" he whispered.

"What?"

"I haven't told anyone yet, not even my parents, so you can't say anything."

My eyes widened. "What is it?"

"Coach thinks there's a possibility I'll get drafted."

My mouth dropped open. "Oh my God. That's amazing."

He nodded, clearly still unable to believe it himself. "Yeah."

"I'm so happy for you."

"I don't want to jinx it, but I needed to tell someone."

"Will you get me tickets?"

"To every game," he assured me. "*If* it happens."

"It will. You're Jordan Grady. You can do anything."

He stared at me long and hard. I couldn't miss the appreciation in his eyes. "Let's go out back."

"Why?"

"Because being in here with you again is making me want to cuddle."

A laugh burst out of me. "You're so stupid."

"I'll take that as a compliment."

I stood. "You shouldn't."

He laughed as he stood, leading us out into the backyard.

"Why do I feel like you're purposely taking me on a walk down memory lane?"

He shrugged. "Can't help it if we share all the same memories."

I followed him into the backyard, the smell of freshly cut grass I'd grown accustomed to thanks to our daily games of catch came rushing back. I walked over to the big tree and ran my hand over the rough bark. The memories flooded my brain. I spun toward him. "I'll never forget you dancing with me that night."

He smiled.

"You really should have taken me." I laughed. "I was so jealous."

He nodded. "That's why I danced with you out here. I never wanted you to feel like second best. Because you weren't. You were always my number one."

Tears snuck out of the corner of my eyes. I quickly swiped them away, but they persisted.

"Em. Don't cry."

I shook my head. "I hate that it's always hanging over us. What I did. I can't erase it. I just wish we could go back to being…us."

He took the two steps necessary to close the space between us and slipped his arms around me, pulling me against his chest. I breathed him in. I embraced the feel of his arms, how much stronger they were than before. I wanted to lose myself in him. "It's gonna take time, but I think we're doing a damn good job. Just know, I want it, too."

I wanted that and more. But how did I say that?

"Hey, look at me."

I tipped my head back and looked up at him with tears staining my cheeks.

"We got this."

I nodded, smiling through my tears.

"Why are you crying?"

Could I just tell him I'd loved him since I was eight?

Could it be that easy?

I shook my head, too scared to ruin everything now that I was just getting it all back.

Jordan's lips turned up into a sad smile. "Let's go sing 'Happy Birthday' and eat some cake before we need to head back to campus."

* * *

Jordan dropped me off just after nine. As I climbed the stairs to my floor, I couldn't help but think about the time spent with the Gradys. It was like being in a time warp, and I was ten-years-old again. The easy laughter filling their kitchen hadn't disappeared. The happiness they exuded in every breath hadn't changed. The love they had for their only son hadn't wavered. They were a real family. And I would've given anything to be part of it.

I walked into my dorm room. Raquel was painting her toenails, feet up on top of her desk. She looked to me with raised brows. "How was your day?"

"As expected." I fell back onto my bed with a sigh.

"What's that mean?"

"It couldn't have been more perfect."

She shook her head. "Why is it that you two aren't screwing like bunnies somewhere right now? Get together already."

I laughed, wishing it were that easy. But with Jordan and me, it's never been that easy.

There was a knock on the door. I sat up as Raquel abandoned her polish and hobbled with wet toenails to the door and opened it.

Flip stood there. "Hey." His eyes searched over her shoulder, and he smiled when he saw me. "You girls up for hanging out? Half the floor's in my room right now. We've got food and beer. And of course soda for you, Emery."

Raquel looked over her shoulder at me with raised brows. "I'm in."

"Me, too," I said, knowing I wouldn't have been able to fall asleep after such a wonderful day with Jordan.

By midnight, lots of alcohol had been consumed by my hall mates and we'd moved on to drinking games.

"Never have I ever…" Flip's roommate Carlos announced from his chair. "…had a threesome."

A few people, including Raquel, lifted their red cups to their lips and drank their beer.

The rest of us laughed, knowing it meant they had indeed been part of a threesome. I apparently had a lot to learn about my roommate.

"Never have I ever…" Sue, a girl from down the hall, said from her spot on the floor. "…been to a strip club."

Most of the guys in the room drank. None of the girls, except Raquel, drank. I laughed to myself. She was definitely full of surprises.

Charlie, a goofy guy from down the hall, jumped in next. "Never have I ever…had sex."

The room went silent before everyone burst out laughing. It was *very* obvious Charlie didn't have any game and hadn't slept with a girl yet. Every one of my hallmates lifted their cups to their mouths and drank…all except Charlie and me.

Most didn't notice I didn't take a sip, but Flip did. I watched his eyes widen with wonder as the information registered.

"My turn," Raquel quickly interjected, glancing briefly to me. "Never have I ever…been in love with one of my friends."

Flip watched me closely as I lifted my cup and sipped my soda. Then he drank his beer, all the while his eyes stayed locked on mine.

Shit.

CHAPTER SEVENTEEN

Grady

I jogged onto the field in Tennessee with my helmet in my hand for our pregame warmup. The Tennessee fans had yet to be let into the massive stadium, and even though they despised us, I needed them there. Their hatred for us gave me a rush. One that made sticking it to them all I wanted to do. I loved coming onto their turf and crushing them. I loved the push it gave me to play like a star. Loved the determination it gave me to pummel anyone in my way.

The grass cushioned each of my steps as I moved out to the fifty-yard line.

"She's a virgin."

I spun around. Flip stood with his helmet in one hand and a football in the other. "What'd you say?"

"Emery. She hasn't given it up yet."

My eyes narrowed on him. What the hell was he trying to do? "So? She's a good girl."

He smirked.

Everything about the guy made my skin crawl. "You can wipe that look off your face."

He lifted his shoulders innocently. "Just wondering how long she's gonna stay that way."

Had we not been on the football field with everyone on our team around, I would've knocked the smirk right off his smug face. But I wasn't gonna let him get into my head. Not when I needed to be focused. I needed to be at my best. "Dude, we're about to play one of our biggest rivals and you're worried about staking your claim on a girl? The word pussy mean anything to you?"

He dropped his helmet and charged at me, shoving me on my ass.

The fuck?

I jumped to my feet and came up swinging like the angry motherfucker he made me. My right hook connected with his face. I heard a crack as his head was thrown to the side, his nose getting some bloody readjusting. But he didn't go down like I expected him to. He came right back at me, blood dripping from his nose as his own fists flew. A lucky left hook caught the corner of my eye. *Son-of-a-bitch.* Before I could retaliate for the cheap shot, my teammates grabbed me from behind and pulled me back, urging me to calm down and back off him.

"What'd I ever do to you, Grady?" Flip asked, as if I attacked *him.*

The bastard's acting chops were stellar.

"Grady!" Coach shouted. "Get on the bench."

I looked to Flip now conveniently cupping his nose with his hand. The team doctors rushed over to him. Of course they did. They needed to check that their fragile golden boy was okay.

I trudged off the field with the skin around my eye swelling up and beginning to throb. I slumped down on the bench. Someone shoved an ice pack at me. I held it to the side of my face for all of two seconds then dropped it to my side. I was no wuss.

"I did *not* say it was okay to hurt him," Coach hissed through clenched teeth as he stood in front of me.

"Whatever," I mumbled like a sullen child, averting his gaze.

"*Whatever?* Is that what you're gonna say when I bench your ass?"

I glared up at him. "You wouldn't."

"Wanna call my bluff?"

I sat there stewing. I did not start that out there. But fucking Flip did a damn good job of making it look that way. Was he that intimidated by me? Or was his beef with me *really* over Emery?

"Put ice on that before you can't see out of it," Coach ordered, before storming away from me.

Abbott took a seat next to me. "Dude. You gotta relax."

"Dude," I said mimicking him. "You gotta back the fuck off me."

"All I'm saying is if we all fought you every time *you* said something to piss us off, we never would've been a cohesive unit over the past three years. Guys say shit. They say shit to piss each other off. Then they move on."

"I hate him."

"Maybe so. But we're relying on *him* to take us to the big game like Caden did. If you keep messing with him, you're gonna ruin it for all of us. And dude, I need us to win." Abbott stood up, purposely letting his words sit with me as he walked onto the field.

As shitty as it was to admit, these guys were at Alabama for a reason. This was their stepping stone to the pros. I couldn't let my hatred for Flip ruin the way I played. Because if I screwed up, I screwed it up for everyone. Including myself.

At three-thirty the whistle blew and the game began. I shut out all the voices in my head. I heard the cheers of Tennessee and let the cheers propel me to the next level. I played the game of my life. My hatred for Flip turned me into a beast out there, pouncing on anyone who moved in my way. By halftime, I'd silenced the Tennessee fans. Okay, so maybe I wasn't the only one doing a good job. But without me, Flip—and his taped-up nose—would've been useless. He sucked under pressure and they were gunning for him. Without me there, he would've been sacked ten times over. Though I'd be lying if I said I didn't want him to eat grass at least once.

We ended up winning by fourteen. Music blared in our locker room after the game. The guys' elation was evident in the laughter and jeering filling the room. Still pissed about the fight with Flip, I snuck away from the celebration, showering and dressing in my own space.

I slid into my seat on the bus a short while later, lifting the armrest and spreading out so I didn't have to share my seat with anyone else. I slipped on my headphones and pulled out my phone to find music to sleep to. Before I could find anything, a text lit up my screen.

You were amazing out there.

I grinned like a fool as my fingers typed out a response. **That's not the only place I'm amazing.**

The three dots appeared for a second. **Ewwwww.**

I laughed and a few of the guys seated around me glanced over as I typed my response. **Just playing.**

I know. Have a safe trip home.

I stared down at the text imagining Emery's excitement while watching the game on television. When we were younger, she'd jump out of her seat and scream for me, not caring who saw her. I always loved that about her.

I switched my music on and let the sounds drown out the rest of the world. I closed my eyes and reclined my chair as far back as it would go. I teetered on the verge of sleep as the bus lurched, pulling away from the stadium. Someone walking down the aisle slammed into my elbow on the armrest. My eyelids flew open and my head came up. Flip stood there, his eye bruised and nose swollen.

I motioned to my own nose. "You got a little something on your face."

"Fuck you."

"Maybe rethink your words. Last time you brought up fucking you got yourself a nice souvenir."

"Grady!" Coach was turned around in his front seat and partially standing. "Enough! Caruso, find a seat."

Flip moved down the aisle and I didn't see him again for the almost five-hour drive back to campus. Just the way I wanted it.

CHAPTER EIGHTEEN

Emery

I grabbed my shower bucket and headed into the hallway, knowing I was going to be late for class if I didn't hurry.

"Emery," Flip called from down the hall.

I spun around, my eyes stretching wide as I took in his swollen nose and black and blue eyes. "Rough game?" I asked.

He scoffed. "You didn't watch?"

"No, I did. You guys looked great out there."

"All of us or just Grady?"

My brows inverted. "What's that supposed to mean?"

"You haven't talked to him?"

"Since you guys got back? No."

"So, you didn't hear he attacked me before the game?"

My mouth dropped open. "What?"

He motioned toward his face. "You think I did this to myself?"

I took in his swelling and bruising. Flashbacks of my mom over the years flooded my brain. Only, she blamed her marks on walking into a wall or tripping over a chair. But I knew the truth. And the mere recollection turned my stomach. "Why would he do that?" I asked, my voice hushed for fear of what he'd say.

"Beats the hell outta me. The guy's a loose cannon."

"So, he hit you for no reason?"

He shrugged. "He hates me."

"He doesn't just hate people. He also doesn't just let people in. You have to earn that."

"Sounds like you're making excuses for him."

I shook my head. "I'm just trying to understand. Growing up he didn't hit people for no reason."

"So, you're taking his side?"

I shook my head. "No, I'm pissed he'd lay a hand on you. It's never okay to hurt someone."

"I'm worried he could hurt you."

I sucked in a sharp breath, sickened by even the thought of it. "He'd *never* hurt me."

"How well do you know him, Emery?" Flip motioned to his face. "Would the guy you know do this to someone?"

Flip's words stayed with me as I showered. So did the damage Jordan had done to his face. *Did* I know Jordan like I thought I did? Had I been so blinded by having him back in my life that I hadn't realized that he wasn't the boy I'd fallen for? Did this Jordan use violence to settle his disputes? He, of all people, knew what that did to people.

* * *

I threw my bag's strap across my chest and headed toward the stairwell. Calculus had been exhausting. Did anyone really need all that math?

I stepped outside, caught up with the bodies moving to their next classes. It was overcast, and as I crossed campus, dark clouds rolled in—such a parallel to my mood. Flip's words still haunted me. Still had me questioning everything. I couldn't shake the memories his injuries elicited in me. It was as if I was that little girl again seeing my mama hurt for no reason. I'd pushed those images away over the past four years, but the fact that Jordan did that to Flip made me sick.

"Em."

A cold shudder shot up my spine. That had never happened before when I heard Jordan's voice. I contemplated not stopping, but I needed to hear his side. I needed him to make it all make sense to me. So I stopped, causing the rushing students to step around me. I didn't turn around.

Jordan caught up with me. "Hey." He smiled with a hint of black around his eye, but his face looked nothing like Flip's face.

"You happy with yourself?" I asked, anger brewing inside of me.

His brows shot up. "Come again."

"You happy you only ended up with a little bruise?"

He scoffed. "So, I see he already got to you?"

My eyes narrowed. "What's that supposed to mean?"

"What'd he tell you?"

I crossed my arms. "Why don't *you* tell me."

He shook his head. "Nope. I wanna hear the shit he's spewing."

"I thought you saw firsthand what violence does to people?"

"Em, this has nothing to do with your—"

"It has *everything* to do with you knowing better." I held up my fist. "This solves nothing."

"He started it."

"You're not ten."

He gnawed on his bottom lip, stopping himself from saying whatever it was he wanted to say.

"And I don't care who started it. You know better."

He balked. "You can't go around telling me what I can and can't do."

I couldn't have stopped my jaw from dropping even if I wanted to. "I'm starting to see the truth."

"What's that supposed to mean?"

"You're not the guy I thought you were."

"Come on, Em," he pled. "You know me."

I shook my head. "I thought I knew you." I spun around and took off.

"Are you seriously walking away again?" he yelled. "We saw how well that worked out last time!"

I could feel myself getting choked up, but I wouldn't allow it. I didn't do anything wrong. *He* did.

CHAPTER NINETEEN

Emery

I spent a long night studying in the library. I'd wanted to be alone. Wanted to let the silence and old books distract me from my anger at Jordan. But nothing helped. I couldn't understand how he could hurt Flip like that. He knew Flip and I were friends. Hell, he and Flip were teammates. Didn't it matter to him? Did *anything* matter to him?

My phone rang in my back pocket as I entered my dorm room. I slipped it out, half expecting it to be Jordan pleading his case again, but it was my mom. "Hey," I said as soon as I answered the phone.

"Emery?" she said, her hushed voice sending up red flags.

"What's wrong?"

Raquel shot up from her bed where she'd been reading. She watched me as I paced the floor.

"He found me," my mom whispered.

A cold chill ran through my veins. "What?"

"I'm in the hospital."

It was as if the floor dropped out from beneath my feet and I grasped hold of my desk for support. "Are you all right?"

There was silence on her end.

"I'm coming right now."

"It's not safe." Her sniffles carried through the phone. "They didn't catch him."

Silent teardrops slipped out of my eyes. "What did he do to you?"

Raquel jumped up and threw a sweatshirt over her pajamas. She stepped into her flip-flops, grabbed her car keys from her desk, and stood by the door. "I'll take you," she whispered.

"I'm coming," I told my mom. "I'll be on the next flight out of here."

My mother said nothing.

She's all I had left in this world and *he* tried to take her from me. "I love you, Mom."

"Love you too. I'm on the fifth floor. You'll see the police officer."

I switched off my phone and searched the room for what I might need.

"I know there are things I don't know about you yet," Raquel said. "But I know you need to get to her right now. So, grab what you need and I'll take you to the airport."

With a hazy mind and tears that wouldn't cease, I grabbed my wristlet, and we rushed down to her car in the student lot. As Raquel sped to the airport, I sat motionless staring out at the dark streets. Thoughts whirled around my head. What had Wayne done to her? What was he *trying* to do? How long had he been searching for her? For us? Was he trying to kill her? I teetered between despair and anger as tears fell.

"My mother was in an abusive relationship," I finally said to Raquel as I stared into the darkness outside my window.

"Oh, *Emery*."

"We got away from him four years ago. But somehow he found her."

"My God. I'm so sorry."

Not as sorry as I was that I'd left my mom alone in Arizona. Left her so I could chase a boy.

Raquel took the exit toward the airport.

My eyes finally cut to hers. "Thank you for being here for me."

"We're roommates. Which makes us friends. Which makes your problems my problems," she assured me as she followed the signs to departures and pulled up to the departure doors.

I pushed open the car door and jumped out with nothing but the clothes on my back and my wristlet holding my ID, an emergency credit card, and a few dollars. I just hoped there was a departing flight soon.

"I'm gonna park and then I'll wait with you," Raquel said.

"They won't let you past the security check-in. I'll be fine."

Her brows lifted. "Will you?"

I shrugged, the most honest answer I could give her. "I'll call you."

She nodded sadly as I closed the door and ran through the sliding doors into the airport. After speaking with representatives at three different airlines, I finally found a flight leaving in twenty minutes. They weren't sure I'd make it through security and to the terminal before the gate closed, but I assured them I would.

I ran through the airport, my hair trailing behind me as if in the midst of a wind storm. I arrived at the gate as they were about to close the door. I held up my ticket. "Wait!"

And just like in the movies, they let me on.

The three-and-a-half-hour flight felt like it lasted days as I sat squished between two larger men whose bodies inched into my space. I was screaming on the inside as my foot tapped wildly beneath me. All I needed was to be with my mom. I needed to know she'd be okay. Know she forgave me for leaving her.

Since I'd brought no luggage, once the plane landed and we filed off the plane, I ran straight for the exit and stepped out onto the sidewalk searching for my car service. The hot Arizona air hit me, reminding me of the past four years spent in the state. Alabama had a breeze from time to time. Arizona's heat stole your breath away.

Once I found my driver, I settled into the back of his car and verified my destination with him. My legs bounced as he drove toward the hospital; I felt ready to jump out of my skin. I hadn't thought to bring a hat—or anything else that would conceal my identity. Wayne had been crazy enough to track down my mom and hurt her. He was crazy enough to be staking out the hospital waiting for me to show up.

My heart thumped at triple speed by the time we pulled up to the hospital entrance. I needed to see my mom. I needed to see what Wayne had done to put her in the hospital. "I know this is an odd question," I said to the driver, as I assessed the area around the entrance. "But is there any way you could walk inside with me?"

His eyes narrowed in question at me through the rearview mirror.

"Someone hurt my mom. That's why she's here. I'm worried he may be—"

The driver threw open his door without letting me finish. "Of course."

I released a breath, realizing kind people still existed in this world. "Thank you."

We rushed into the lobby and right to the elevators. The driver stood with me as I waited for the doors to split apart. Once they did and we saw the elevator was empty, I stepped inside. "Thank you," I said to him as the doors closed me inside.

As I stood alone, the elevator music sounded muffled, like I was under water. My weary reflection in the mirrored walls blurred as if in the throes of a horrible nightmare. The truth was, I *was* in a horrible nightmare. The wait was torture. Please don't stop on another floor, I prayed.

The elevator bell chimed and I held my breath.

The doors split apart.

I saw that I was on the fifth floor and released my breath.

I dashed out into the empty hallway, searching left and right until I spotted the uniformed police officer seated outside the last room on the right.

He glanced up, quickly jumping to his feet and meeting me halfway down the hallway. "Emery?"

I nodded.

"Your mom said you'd be coming."

"How is she?"

"She had a rough go at it. But she survived."

"Survived?"

He nodded. "It was bad. But she's a tough woman."

"She is," I said. "And him?" The words dripped from my mouth with as much hatred as I felt.

"He left her for dead. Our best men are working on it."

Vomit roiled up my throat. I was a terrible daughter. A *selfish* daughter. I'd abandoned my mother for Alabama. For Jordan. "I should've been there. I should've protected her."

"Then you'd be in the bed beside her," he assured me. "She did a good job fending him off long enough to send an emergency call from her phone. He probably heard our sirens and ran for it."

"Can I see her?"

He nodded. "She's been in and out of consciousness all day. They have her on heavy pain meds." He stepped aside so I could continue down the hallway.

My feet felt like they were submerged in quicksand as I approached her room, each step becoming more difficult. The sterile hospital scent singed the inside of my nose. The shaking in my hands had nothing on the fear I had of seeing her. I dragged in a deep breath and stepped inside the room.

My mother slept under white sheets with only her face visible. It was good she was asleep because I couldn't hide my horror. Her face was entirely black and blue and swollen. If I didn't know it was her, she would've been unrecognizable. Vomit again crept up the back of my throat as I took in the sight of my poor battered mother. Tears glazed my eyes. Rage I didn't know I was capable of feeling spread through me.

I approached her bed slowly and lowered myself into the empty chair beside her, transfixed on the damage Wayne had done.

I reached under the sheet and took her cold limp hand into mine. An IV was attached to the back of it, connected to a drip bag at her side. "I'm here, Mama."

My mother's eyes cracked open, and her head fell to the side on her pillow. She tried to smile but winced at the pain it caused her.

"Don't say anything. I'm here now. Just rest."

"I stood up to him," she whispered.

I fought back the tears stinging my eyes and did my best to smile. "I know you did."

She closed her eyes, and the even sound of her breathing indicated sleep.

Tears streamed down my cheeks as I watched her sleep. What had she done to deserve a man like that? She'd once told me he swept in to rescue her after my real father died. She must have been so blinded by grief she didn't see him for the man he was—a drunk with a violent temper. But that description no longer fit him. Finding her in Arizona and attacking her had been premeditated. There was no excuse. He couldn't blame it on the alcohol. He'd plotted this. That made him a monster.

But where was he now?

The longer I sat there clutching my mother's hand, the angrier I became. My tears subsided and my mind became clouded with revenge. With payback. With the pain I wanted inflicted on him. I was such a hypocrite. I'd shamed Jordan for using his fist on Flip, and now that's all I wanted someone to do to Wayne. If not more.

Between the anger and the exhaustion, my eyelids eventually grew heavy.

An hour passed, and my pursuit to resist sleep failed me. I just needed to rest my head. I just needed to close my eyes for a minute. I lowered my head down on the bed.

I just needed a minute…

CHAPTER TWENTY

Emery

A hand cupped my shoulder. I jerked up and spun in my chair.

Jordan stood in the dark hospital room beside me, his eyes on my mother.

"What are you doing here?" I asked, my voice groggy with sleep.

"Is she okay?" he said, squatting down beside the chair so not to wake her.

"He found her."

His jaw clenched, and the ticking there made his anger palpable. "I should've killed him when I had the chance."

"*Jordan.*"

"No, Em." He gave me a sidelong glance. "I begged my parents to get him out of your house."

"You did?"

"Of course I did. When the sheriff showed up, your mom told them everything was okay."

"She did?"

I could see the anger brewing in his eyes, and I thought maybe it would break him. "My parents said if he didn't hurt you—and your mom wanted him there, there was nothing else they could do."

I nodded, knowing if he thought for one minute Wayne had ever touched me, he would have killed him.

"You should've called me. I shouldn't have found out from your roommate."

"She shouldn't have contacted you."

"Right. *You* should have. Best friends are there for each other. You knew that at one time."

"Are we really gonna do this here?" I was too exhausted to argue with him. Too exhausted to even be mad at him for what happened with Flip.

He closed his eyes, shame marring his features. "I'm sorry. I was just so scared when she told me. I was scared you were next."

"I'm safe here. There's a police officer."

A long silence passed between us. My mother and I lived a terrible life with Wayne. And even though we'd escaped him, we were constantly looking over our shoulders. Now, that he was out there, we were like sitting ducks and I had no idea what to do about it.

"Jordan?" my mother whispered.

Jordan jumped up and grabbed her hand from mine. "I'm right here, Ma'am. Can I get you something?"

Her words were soft and slow. "Thank you for being here for Emery."

He glanced to me sadly before looking back to her. "I'll always be here for Emery. And *you*."

"Mom, do you need me to get the doctor?" I asked.

"I just need to sleep," she said.

"Then rest. I'll be here when you wake up."

Her eyes closed, and the soft purrs of sleep escaped her once again.

"She's on a lot of pain meds," I explained.

"Can I get you something?" he asked. "A drink? Some food?"

I shook my head. "I'm so tired, but I don't want her to wake up and not have me awake."

He ticked his head to the empty bed in the room. "Go sleep. I'll sit with her."

"Are you serious? You've been up all night too."

"I slept on the plane."

Maybe if I slept for a little while longer, I'd be able to coherently speak with the doctors and detectives in the morning. "You sure?"

"Of course."

I pushed myself to my feet. Jordan unexpectedly grabbed hold of my hand and pulled me into his chest, wrapping his arms around me and pressing his lips to the crown of my head. "Everything's gonna be all right."

I nodded, hoping more than anything he was right. I let him hold me. But the longer I stayed folded in his arms, the longer I wanted to stay there. The safety he provided, and the way even at my lowest he made me feel as if everything was going to be all right, was what our relationship had been based on. But I couldn't always let him rescue me. I had to be strong on my own.

I stepped out of his arms. "I'll only sleep for a little bit." I moved to the empty bed on the other side of the room. I was too tired to even pull back the sheets, so I laid on top of them, curling myself into a ball and hugging my knees.

"Take all the time you need," Jordan said softly before sleep carried me under once again.

Grady

I sat in the chair and took hold of Emery's mom's hand. I wanted her to know someone was with her. Sadly, between the bruising and swelling, you couldn't see the attractive woman she was.

There were so many things I wanted to say to her. So many things I should have done to prevent what happened.

"Jordan." Her eyes cracked open.

"Ma'am?"

"She missed you," she whispered.

"I know," I said, leaning closer so she didn't have to strain her voice to talk to me.

"I didn't let her contact you."

"Water under the bridge," I assured her. "You just need to get better."

"Will you take care of her if anything happens to me?"

Fucking tears pricked my eyes. "Nothing's gonna happen to you. Just focus on getting better."

Her eyes closed as she drifted back off to sleep. Did she really think she might not make it? Were her internal wounds more severe than we knew? And what about Emery? If anything happened to her mom, would she even let me take care of her?

"How's she doing?" a voice asked.

I spun in my chair to find the police officer standing inside the doorway.

I shrugged. "She's in and out of sleep."

"Terrible thing that happened to her."

"He was a monster when we were kids."

He nodded, staring at her battered body.

"What's being done to catch him?" I asked.

The officer's eyes moved back to me. "We've got men on it. But the guy could be anywhere by now."

"Could he get in here?"

He shook his head. "His picture's plastered all over every nurses' station, bathroom, and entrance in this place."

"Doesn't mean he won't find a way. He tracked her down in another state."

He tapped the gold badge on the front of his shirt. "That's why I'm here."

"But for how long? And what happens when she gets out of here? Who will protect her then?"

"All valid questions."

"Does that mean you don't have the answers?"

"Sorry."

I nodded. It wasn't his fault. But I wanted those answers. Who *would* ensure her safety? And Emery's?

The officer walked back out to his post, and I slipped my phone from my pocket, sending my uncle Cal a text. He had a law firm in Montgomery and always came through for me when I needed him. Hence the private jet and pilot he lent me to get to Arizona at a minute's notice. He asked only that I call when I figured out the situation. Then he could provide legal counsel.

CHAPTER TWENTY-ONE

Emery

Sunlight yanked me from a restless sleep. My eyes parted and the bright room around me instantly reminded me where I was and why I was there. I sat up. Jordan sat beside my mom, his hand clasping hers. He watched her while she slept, his eyes heavy with sleep.

"Did she wake up?" I asked, turning so my legs hung off the side of the bed.

He looked to me. "A couple times."

I nodded, not knowing what to say to him in the light of day. "You didn't have to come."

"Say it again and I'll…"

"You'll what?"

"I'll come over there."

I scoffed. "Is that supposed to scare me?"

He placed my mom's hand down by her side on top of the sheet and stood, his tall body moving toward me.

I sat still, braced for his attempt at intimidation. "Still not scared."

He stopped at the side of my bed and stared down at me. He said nothing, but I could tell he was taking in my puffy eyes and the creases around them—the result of lack of sleep and fear. Fear of Wayne. Fear of the unknown. Fear of losing the people I loved most in the world. He wrapped his arms around me and pulled me into his chest.

I pushed down the tears that sat at the ready as I breathed in his scent, then pulled back from him. "Don't."

His face scrunched. "Don't what?"

"Don't swoop in to save the day like you used to."

He stepped back and crossed his arms. "Why the hell not?"

"Because you can't be one guy with me and then hurt people when I'm not around."

"This is about Flip?"

"This is about you. This is about you changing and me…well, me thinking you would've stayed the same."

"You're not making any sense. I'm the same guy I always was."

I cocked my head, challenging his words.

Anger replaced his sympathy. "So, you don't want me here?"

"I don't know. Why *are* you here?"

"Because I'm your best friend. I show up when you need me and punch guys to protect your honor."

I rolled my eyes.

He threw his arms out to his sides, frustration emanating from his body. "What, Em? What do you want from me?"

I shook my head, not wanting to answer.

"Tell me. What do you want?"

"Nothing."

"Liar."

I sucked in a sharp breath.

"Now I'll ask you again. What do you want?"

"I want *you*," I blurted, the words tumbling out before I could stop them. I clasped my mouth with my hand. *Shit.*

His head whipped back. "What?"

I hated my lack of control with him around. I dropped my hand. "You heard me," I grumbled like a sullen child.

"Jesus, Em."

"It's not like you didn't know."

"Of course I didn't know. I mean, I knew you were crushing on me as a kid, but…"

"But what?"

He shrugged, and for the first time ever, he was at a loss for words.

"Is it that hard to envision?"

"What? No." He moved closer, cupping my cheeks with his hands as he looked intensely at me. "You're the most beautiful girl I know. I just…"

My gaze dropped from his. This wasn't how I wanted all this to play out. My emotions were just so out of whack after what happened to my mom, my lack of sleep, and him showing up. "Just forget I said anything."

"Forget it?"

"Emery?" my mother called softly from the bed.

I flew out of Jordan's grasp and made my way into the chair beside my mom. "I'm right here, Mama." I grasped her frail hand. "How are you doing? Can I get you something? Should I get the doctor?"

"Slow down," she said.

"I'll get the doc," Jordan said as he moved to the door and disappeared in the hallway.

"Have they caught Wayne?" she asked.

I shook my head. "Not that I've heard."

She closed her swollen eyes, and I could see the pain of what she'd endured. "There was knocking on the door. I should've known better than to open it without looking."

"Mom, it's not your fault. He's a sick man."

"When I saw him standing there, I knew it was over. I knew he was going to kill me."

Tears pooled in my eyes. "Mama, save your energy. It's not good to think about it. You survived."

"I just need you to know. I just need you to be aware. He could come for you. And the thought is destroying me." Tears fell freely from her eyes and streamed down her swollen cheeks.

I cupped her hand in both of mine. "I'll be fine."

"I won't let anything happen to her," Jordan assured my mom from the doorway.

"Thank you," she said to him.

"The doctor's on his way," Jordan said.

I was too embarrassed to look over my shoulder at him, though I wondered how much of our conversation he'd heard. "I think the swelling's going down a little."

"You've always been a terrible liar," she said.

"Yeah," Jordan added. "Remember when she threw the baseball and broke the vinyl siding on Esther's house and blamed that kid down the street?"

My mom smiled, though I could see it hurt her to do it.

"And how about the time she—" he continued.

"Okay. We get it," I said. "I'm a terrible liar."

"Marisa?" A doctor in a white coat walked in holding my mom's chart. "I'm Doctor Vickers. How are you doing?"

"I'm having some discomfort," she admitted.

Jordan left the room to give us privacy.

"That's to be expected," the doctor said. "From what they tell me, you're lucky you called the police when you did."

I squeezed her hand gently.

"It appears as though there was some internal bleeding due to the ecchymosis on your abdomen." He glanced to me. "The purple skin tells me there's bleeding into the skin and soft tissue. We're using intravenous fluids to prevent any drop in blood pressure."

I nodded, trying to keep up. "That's good, right?"

"Well, she's still under observation. She's scheduled for an ultrasound to check if the bleeding has slowed or, ideally, has corrected itself." He glanced back to my mom. "Are you having pain anywhere else?"

"In my side when I move or take a deep breath," she admitted.

"Broken ribs," he asserted. "We'll do an X-ray to be sure you don't have a pneumothorax." He glanced to me. "A punctured lung."

He looked back to my mom. "Anything else?"

"My right arm." She spoke softly. "He slammed me into a wall."

Anger coursed through my body. Childhood memories rushed through my mind. The darkness in his eyes. The despair in hers.

"We have people here you can talk to," the doctor offered. "The physical wounds will heal. That's what I'm here for. It's the ones left inside—the emotional ones— we need to be sure are healing."

My mother said nothing, but I could tell she was thinking a thousand things as tears welled in her eyes.

Tears pricked my own eyes. "Thank you, Doctor," I answered for my mom, hating to see her so uncomfortable. "Please excuse me for a sec." I released her hand and stood, walking unsteadily into the hallway to compose myself and give her time alone with the doctor.

I moved past the new police officer seated in the chair outside the door, making it halfway down the hallway before stopping and leaning against the wall. I closed my eyes and dropped my head back, needing to catch my breath.

Hearing her say she thought he was going to kill her shook me to the core. Heinous visions of what she must've been through raced through my mind. Him slamming her into the wall. Him leaving her for dead? What happened in between? How had she endured internal bleeding? How had her ribs been broken? How could he leave her that way?

"You okay?"

I didn't need to open my eyes to know it was Jordan who'd moved beside me. "I have no idea."

His hand slipped into mine. "Whatever you need."

I opened my eyes and turned my head so I could see him. "I can't leave her."

His gaze cut to mine. "I know."

Tears blurred my vision. "I can't even begin to imagine what happened in that house."

"Em, don't go there." He stepped away from the wall to face me, holding my hand and caging me in with his body. "It won't help anyone."

"I hate him, Jordan. He deserves the worst kind of fate."

"And he'll get it. They've got the entire police department out looking for him."

I scoffed, knowing he was probably already back wherever he'd been living.

"Don't. The Emery I knew always looked at the glass half full. Karma will come for him. If not today, soon. I assure you of that."

"I left her," I muttered, my chest tightening around my heart.

"You followed your dream."

"I followed you."

His body stiffened and sadness shone in his eyes. "Are we gonna talk about what happened back there?"

"Do we have to?"

"Yeah, we do." He lifted his fingertips to my hairline and brushed my hair back from my face.

The intimate gesture would've sent my heart racing had I not known the truth. He was only trying to make me feel better. About my mom. About me thoroughly embarrassing myself. About him rejecting me.

"But right now," he continued, his eyes softening at the corners, "You should get back in there and be there for your mom. She needs you." He stepped back, giving me space.

"Yeah." I slipped my hand free from his and moved away from the wall.

Jordan disappeared after our hallway encounter, claiming he needed to make some calls since he'd already missed practice back in Alabama. But I wondered if he just didn't know what to say to me. I didn't blame him. I wasn't making a whole lot of sense. One minute I hated what he did to Flip. The next I'm confessing my love for him. It was surprising he hadn't hopped onto the next plane out of Arizona.

Maybe he had.

I spent the majority of the day sitting with my mom— when she wasn't off having tests done. The nurses kept me abreast of her results. The internal bleeding had ceased, but, like the doctor assumed, she suffered three broken ribs and a broken arm. While my mom slept in the late afternoon, I spent time with the detectives in charge of her case. They assured me they'd find Wayne and promised she'd continue to have twenty-four-hour protection. Though, they were unable to tell me what would happen once she was discharged from the hospital.

"Hope you're hungry," Jordan said when he finally returned around dinner time.

I turned from the chair beside my mom to find him carrying a tray piled high with clear plastic food containers.

"I wasn't sure what you might want, so I—"

"Bought one of everything?" I asked.

He glanced down at the tray, before holding it out for me to see. "Yup."

I grabbed a turkey wrap and soda. "Thank you."

"That's all you want?"

I nodded.

He placed the tray down on the small nightstand between the two beds. He dropped down onto the extra bed and ticked his head toward the empty space beside him.

I looked to my mom who slept soundly, probably due to the extra dose of pain meds added to her drip bag. Jordan grabbed a burger from the tray as I stood and moved to the spot beside him.

We ate in silence. I was embarrassed and uncomfortable. And, the fact that Jordan hadn't reacted how I dreamt he would made an already horrific day worse.

But I couldn't take it back now. It was out there.

"Any new information?" he asked.

I shook my head.

"So, is the police department gonna keep an open line of communication with you?"

I nodded as I bit into my wrap. It had been a lot of information to digest.

My mother's nurse walked into the room. I could tell something was wrong.

"What's wrong?" I asked, bracing myself for more bad news.

"There was a big accident at the car plant two towns away. The ER has been jammed and now we're moving patients into rooms." She lifted her chin toward us. "We need that bed."

My body deflated. "Oh."

"Honey, I know you want to stay with your mom," she said. "But there's a hotel right next door. Why don't you go get a good night's sleep, without the monitors beeping. There's going to be a lot of noise as we get the new patient situated."

I glanced to Jordan. He nodded his agreement.

"Will someone call me if she needs me?" I asked.

"Of course," she assured me. "And the police officer is here as well."

"I'm going with you. Your mom has security." Jordan said. "You've got me."

CHAPTER TWENTY-TWO

Emery

Jordan held the keycard to the sensor on the hotel door. Once it clicked, he pushed the door open. I stepped inside the dark room, switching on the light to find a king-sized bed in the center with a mountain of fluffy white pillows. I glanced accusatorially at him.

He smirked. "There was no way I wasn't sleeping in the same bed as you."

I moved to the bed and lowered myself down onto the edge. "It's been a long time."

"I seriously couldn't have planned this any better myself," he said with a smug grin.

"You mean you didn't pay off that nurse?"

He laughed. "I wish I'd thought of that." He moved to the bed, his smile disappearing as he sat down beside me, the mattress dipping and forcing me into his side. He wrapped his arm around my shoulders and held me close.

"What did your coach say about you missing practice?" I asked.

He shrugged.

"Is he gonna bench you Saturday?"

"He can do whatever he wants."

"You need to go back," I said. "I'll be fine. The door's got multiple locks."

His eyebrows pinched together in the center. "Do you really think that's the only reason I'm staying?"

I shrugged. "You've always been good at helping a friend in need."

He reached over and gripped my chin, turning my face gently toward his. "Em, you're more than just a friend to me."

I swallowed my nerves. "What am I?"

His eyes never wavered from mine. "You're everything good in me."

Taken aback by his words—and suddenly very aware of his closeness—I looked away.

"Don't go getting shy on me now. I need you looking at me when I say this."

My eyes shifted back to his. They stared at me with an intensity I hadn't seen since he was a kid claiming he'd play football at Alabama.

"Em." His hand drifted from my chin to my cheek, cupping it gently. "We've been doing this dance for a long time now. And we were just never at the same place. But we're both here now. You're finally nineteen. And you just told me you've always wanted me—which I've gotta tell you, felt fucking amazing."

Nervous laughter escaped me.

"And I think down deep, even when I couldn't have you, I wanted you too."

A ripple the size of a tsunami rolled through my belly as tears filled my eyes.

"Don't you dare cry on me right now," he said. "I want us, Em. I know my timing sucks with everything going on with your mom, but I couldn't go on letting you think your feelings were one-sided. I'm not entirely sure how this is gonna work, us going from friends to something more, but I want to give it a try."

I chewed on my bottom lip, stopping a big dopey grin from spreading across my face.

"Now I need to know one thing."

"What?"

"Have you kissed Flip because—"

"*Jordan?* I. Don't. Want. Flip."

He was on me before I could blink, his mouth capturing mine. The same numbness that spread through my lips and down my body four years ago surged through me again. I opened my mouth slightly, and his tongue pushed inside, the kiss reaching all the way down to the tips of my toes. His other hand gripped my other cheek and he held me to him as we devoured each other, neither able to get close enough. Before I knew it, his hands dropped from my cheeks to my hips. Our lips stayed connected as he lifted me and dropped me onto his lap. I straddled him, my hands lifting to the back of his head, my fingers tunneling through his hair and holding him to me.

He pulled back slightly, his eyes riveting between mine. "Is this what you want?"

Though my body was a live wire ready to zap everything in a five-mile radius, I shook my head.

Jordan's eyes narrowed, questions brewing behind them.

"*You're* what I want," I said.

He touched his forehead to mine. "And *you're* what I want."

I closed my eyes and let his words wash over me like a warm summer breeze. I wanted them to seep into every one of my pores and burrow there where they belonged. Where they *always* belonged. I opened my eyes to find his trained on mine. "I feel like I've been waiting forever for you to realize that."

"Sorry it took so long."

I pulled back and lifted my fingertips to his cheeks, letting them graze over his skin. Day-old stubble on his jaw tickled the pads on my fingers as they drifted down. "Will you kiss me, Jordan Grady?"

His lips slid into a knowing smirk as his eyes twinkled with amusement. "Like some day?" he asked, the same way he had the first time I asked the question.

I shook my head, loving that he remembered.

He grinned. "Just so we're on the same page, I plan to kiss you whenever and wherever I want from here on out."

I laughed as he buried his mouth in my neck and peppered my collarbone with open-mouthed kisses that sent my eyes crossing. He'd never done that before and the tremors rippling down to my core awoke something inside me. Something I didn't know I'd been missing. I'd promised myself I'd wait for "The One." And there wasn't a doubt in my mind that Jordan Grady was "The One."

But...he was right about our timing. It couldn't have been any worse. And I didn't want our first time marred by the circumstances that had brought us there together.

Jordan pulled back and looked me in the eyes. "Where'd you go?"

"I'm right here."

"You're a terrible liar."

"I want this," I assured him.

He nodded. "Me too."

"But..."

"But it's not happening right now," he said.

I nodded.

"Em, do you think I was gonna try to get you naked in a hotel room with your mom across the way in the hospital?"

I shrugged.

"Okay, so maybe if you let me, I would've," he said with a small grin. "But, I know our timing sucks. And I know there couldn't be a worse time for this to be happening. But I really want to kiss the hell out of you right now."

I tipped my head back and laughed. It felt so good to laugh when the last couple days had been some of the most trying of my life.

"And then," he continued. "I want to sleep next to you all night. Because it's been too damn long since I held my girl."

Butterflies took flight in my belly as I stifled a smile. "Say 'my girl' again."

"My girl."

Emotions rushed through me, snagging my breath away. "I like that."

"You *love* that," he corrected with a grin.

My fingertips moved back to his cheeks and drifted over them, finally understanding what it felt like to get your biggest wish. "Thanks for being you."

He inched closer. "Thanks for making me remember who I am." He captured my lips with his. This kiss was soft and slow and holding so much more than desire and lust. My body relaxed into him as I let him hold me. Let him pull me closer. Let him want me. Eventually, he pulled away, and our breaths mixed, fast and shallow. "Let's get you to sleep."

A huff of disappointment escaped me. But I knew, regardless of my raging hormones, I needed to sleep and forget everything else for a little while. I climbed off Jordan's lap and stood, looking down at him.

He smiled coyly and so much was exchanged in that one smile.

"I really need to shower."

He nodded. "Just know. This is me holding my tongue."

My brows dipped. "Why?"

"Because there are so many things I'd like to say right now pertaining to you and me in that shower."

I snickered. This newfound status change was going to take some getting used to.

I moved to the bathroom and closed the door behind me. My heart flipped summersaults in my chest as I mentally did a happy dance.

Jordan Grady called me his girl and meant it.

Jordan kissed me and meant it.

Gahhhhhhhh.

I stepped in front of the mirror and gaped at my flushed cheeks and tussled ponytail. How could I feel so happy after what happened to my mother? Did that make me a horrible person?

I moved away from the mirror and switched on the shower, peeling off the clothes I'd been wearing since I left Alabama. I tugged my hair free from my elastic and slipped it around my wrist.

I stepped under the spray of the water and just stood there for a long time, thinking about my mom. And Jordan. And leaving Alabama. I needed to be with my mom. Regardless of her trying to be strong, she needed me. I'd let her down once by not being there. I wouldn't make that mistake again. I'd transfer to school in Arizona. I could still attain my dream there. I just wouldn't be doing it with Jordan.

Once I eventually lathered my skin and hair with the hotel soap and shampoo, the water became cooler. I'd been in there longer than I'd wanted to. I switched off the water and dried off with a soft white towel. Not wanting to put my dirty clothes back on, I wrapped another towel around my body and tied my hair into a knot on top of my head.

I checked myself in the mirror one more time, noting my pink cheeks thanks to the hot water and "the Jordan effect," then pulled opened the door.

Jordan had pulled down the comforter and sheets and sat on the edge of the bed in nothing but his boxers, waiting for me. "I wasn't sure what side you wanted."

I smiled. "What's with the gentleman act?"

"You wouldn't think I was a gentleman if you could hear what I'm thinking right now seeing you in that towel," he said, a devious glint in his eyes.

I chuckled as I lifted my chin toward the bed. "You get in first. I'll take this side."

He climbed under the sheets and turned on his side, resting his head in his palm as he watched me climb in.

I turned on my side away from him. If I was going to get any sleep, I needed to *not* be looking at him.

His arms slipped around my waist and he pulled me against his bare chest. I closed my eyes and reveled in the nostalgia washing over me. It had been four years since he held me that way. I'd missed being in his arms, missed it so damn much. His heartbeat reverberated off my back, practically in sync with mine. We lay like that for a long time, both of us undoubtedly having the same thoughts.

He buried his nose in my hair. "Feels like home."

My belly rippled something fierce. "Because it is."

And as much as I wanted to stay awake and lose myself in the feel of being in Jordan's arms again, the security he provided allowed sleep to pull me under and fill my mind with beautiful dreams.

CHAPTER TWENTY-THREE

Grady

I awoke to a dark room, the bedside clock reading six a.m. Emery lay in my arms in the same position we'd fallen asleep. It was as if I'd been transported to my childhood bedroom. Only now, she was naked under her towel. I pressed my lips to her bare shoulder, wishing our circumstances were different. We hadn't discussed the fact that she'd be staying in Arizona, but I knew her. She wouldn't leave her mom again.

So, where'd that leave us?

Bringing it up seemed like a terrible idea. It would only ruin what had happened between us, and there was no way in hell I was gonna be the one to do that.

I thought about her towel and couldn't resist. I leaned down and peppered her bare shoulders with soft kisses, her skin satin to my chapped lips.

"Mmmmm," she murmured as I created a path to the nape of her neck, tracing my tongue up and down the dip beneath her hairline.

"Ahhhh," she breathed.

I teased her a little more before abandoning that spot and tracing a path of open-mouthed kisses across her back.

Without warning, she twisted in my arms. "You need to stop."

"Why?"

Her sleepy smile was a welcome vision. "Because it feels so good."

I chuckled before dropping kisses all over her face. "If you thought that felt good, wait until we get back to school where I'll have you all to myself."

"*If* I go back to school."

"*When* you go back to school," I repeated.

Time seemed to stall as I could tell she was thinking some serious thoughts. "Promise?"

"Promise," I assured her.

She buried her head against my chest and sighed.

Never in a million years, when that tiny eight-year-old showed up at my window, had I thought this was how we'd end up. But now that we had, I didn't want to do a damn thing to ruin it.

"I have an idea," I said.

"What?" she asked, her head beneath my chin.

"I'll tell you when I get it all worked out. In the meantime, there's something I need to tell you."

She pulled back so she could see me and I watched her swallow down hard. "What?"

"I need you to know why I punched Flip."

She released a slow breath, clearly expecting something much worse. "Fine," she said.

"He told me you were a virgin."

She flinched.

"He was trying to get to me, like he knew something personal about you, which I guess he thought would make me think you told him things you didn't tell me."

"We were playing Have You Ever," she explained. "And it just came out."

"It's not your fault. And believe me, I tried to avoid him, but he kept pushing. Then he said something like he wondered how long you'd stay that way."

She gasped.

"He wanted me to think he was gonna take your virginity."

I watched as the blood drained from her face.

"So, I punched him," I continued, needing her to know everything. "And he made it look like I started it, so Coach was pissed at me. The guy's a snake, Em. I just want you to know who you're hanging with."

"Who I *hung* with," she said. "I'm sorry I didn't hear you out. That was wrong of me."

A cocky smile pulled up the corner of my mouth. "I'd say you've made it up to me."

Her brows shot up. "Oh, yeah?"

I pushed forward and rolled her onto her back, covering her with my body. "Definitely wouldn't be opposed to you trying to make it up to me some more, though."

She couldn't respond because my lips captured hers.

When I finally pulled away, I said, "Let's stop at that store across the street and grab you some clothes before we head back. You've been wearing yours since Alabama."

"So, that's your idea?"

"Nope. I'm full of them, baby."

She laughed, and I loved that I had that effect on her.

I leaned down and buried my lips where her neck met her shoulder. I teased her with kisses that turned her laughter into quiet moans that would undoubtedly leave me hard as a rock for the foreseeable future.

* * *

I grabbed Emery's hand as we walked out of the store with a bag full of clothes and a new outfit on her. While she'd been in the changing room, I'd been able to secure the surprise I hoped I could give her. We made our way across the street and the second we stepped into the hospital parking lot, her body tensed.

"What's wrong?"

She looked around the crowded lot, as if expecting to find something there. "Nothing."

"Em. This is me. Talk to me."

"Wayne," she whispered. "I keep expecting him to appear."

I released her hand and wrapped my arm around her shoulders, pulling her into my side as we continued to walk. "I'm here. Nothing's gonna happen to you."

"How can you be sure?"

"Because I know Wayne. And I know what a coward he is. He doesn't fight men. He fights women because he's stronger than they are. That's the sign of a coward."

"He's stronger than me," she admitted.

"It's not gonna come to that," I assured her. But could I really be sure? I wouldn't be with her twenty-four hours a day. Maybe I could convince her to train in the gym with me. "I'll teach you how to defend yourself."

She balked.

"I'm serious. We'll make sure that coward never lays a finger on you or anyone else for that matter ever again."

She said nothing the rest of the way up to her mother's room. I wondered if she believed me or if she just thought I was trying to make her feel better.

Emery's somber mood changed once we stepped into her mother's room. And despite the patient on the other side of the curtain in the center of the room, Em's mom still had the privacy she needed to heal. "Hi, Mama," Emery said.

Her mother was sitting up in bed watching television and she gave us a small smile. "You're back."

Emery sat in the chair beside the bed. "You look so much better."

"I feel better. The doctor said I could be released in a few days."

Emery's eyes expanded and instead of shining with excitement, they were filled with fear. "A few days? You can't go back home."

"She's not," I announced as I placed my hand on Emery's shoulder. "She's going to my parent's house."

Emery and her mother looked to me confused. "What?"

"I spoke to them this morning." I glanced to Emery. "You heard what my dad said. My mom needs something to do. And there's nothing she loves more than taking care of people."

"I couldn't," Emery's mother said.

"Why not?" I asked. "She's excited to have you. But she knows it's only until you get back on your feet and find a place of your own that's safe."

"This is your idea?" Emery asked, almost unable to believe it.

I nodded. "Your mom will be taken care of and close to you." I squeezed her shoulder. "You won't have to leave school. It's a win for everyone."

Appreciation shone in Emery's eyes. And something about that look made me want to do more things to get her to look at me that way. She looked to her mother. "Would it be something you'd be willing to consider?"

Indecision flashed in her mom's eyes.

I wanted to say whatever I could to convince her it was the right decision. I couldn't lose Em again.

"The Gradys are wonderful people," Em continued. "You know that Mama. They love me and care about you too."

She sat silent for several seconds. "Can I think about it?"

Emery nodded. "Whatever you need, Mama."

"Would it be okay if I spoke to your mom?" she asked me.

"Yeah. Of course. But let me warn you. She's gonna try tempting you with promises of fresh dumplings. They're her specialty."

"It's been a while since I've had southern cooking," she said with a smile.

That gave me hope my plan just might work after all.

Emery

I stood by the sliding doors of the hospital lobby with Jordan's arms around me.

"Do I need to worry about you?" he asked into the crown of my head.

I shook my head against his chest. "You already threatened every cop who would listen that they needed to escort me to and from the hotel."

He laughed. "Damn straight I did."

The thought of being there alone, with Wayne still out there somewhere, filled my body with fear.

"I'll see you in a week," he assured me.

I nodded.

"Everything's gonna be fine. Isn't that what you said before forcing me to get back to campus?"

I stepped out of his arms and gave him a brave smile. "Yes. I'll be fine."

He stared at me and I wondered if he was looking for a sign that I was lying. But I wouldn't cave. He needed to get back to school. And he needed to play football. "I'll be at the airport when you get back," he finally said. "Should I bring a sign?"

"A sign?" I laughed. "You're so stupid."

"Why?"

"Because I couldn't miss you in a crowd of thousands."

CHAPTER TWENTY-FOUR

Emery

The week dragged by. I missed all my classes and, more importantly, I missed Jordan. We'd spoken every day, but it wasn't the same as having him there with me. The positive side was my mama had gotten stronger. And she was heading home with me—or at least to the Grady's. And that was all that mattered.

The police hadn't located Wayne, so security remained a huge concern for both of us. But Jordan's uncle Cal had worked his legal magic and secured twenty-four-hour protection outside the Grady's home. A police car would be a beacon alerting Wayne of her whereabouts, so he arranged for an unmarked vehicle with a plain-clothes officer to be parked nearby until Wayne was caught.

There'd been talk of hiring security for me on campus, but because I'd never been a target for Wayne *and* security on campus was tight, I was allowed to return. Jordan's uncle met with the dean and campus security. They decided I needed to travel to and from classes with another person, and I was never allowed to be alone outside of my dorm room.

As our plane landed in Alabama, I gathered our belongings—pretty much what we had on our backs and the few items Jordan and I had bought at the store in Arizona. Since the house was no longer a crime scene,

Jordan offered to go grab my mom's belongings, but she didn't want him to. I wondered if she worried about what he'd see.

We waited for the other passengers to disembark, then I helped my mom off the plane. I grabbed a wheelchair and wheeled her past the luggage claim and out to the lobby.

I glanced around the crowded area. There were people reuniting with loved ones and people saying their goodbyes. My heartbeat stuttered when I spotted Jordan standing there. A smooth smile slipped across his face when he spotted me. He didn't hold the sign he teased me about as he strolled toward us empty-handed.

My heart thumped in tandem with his steps.

When he finally reached us, he leaned down to my mom first and hugged her, which just made me adore him more. "How are you feeling?" he asked her.

"Good, honey. Thank you for everything."

He stepped back from my mom. "You might want to look away for a minute," he told her. "I intend to kiss your daughter until she forgets her name."

She laughed as she looked away, taking in the scenery in the opposite direction to give us the moment Jordan requested.

Jordan swept me right off my feet. "Hi," he said, his nose rubbing playfully against mine.

I wrapped my arms around him. "Hi."

His lips found mine and, for the first time since he'd returned to Alabama, I could breathe easier. His tongue licked its way into my mouth and tangled with mine. I didn't even care people passed by us—or that my mom was right there. I was caught up in the moment. Caught up in Jordan's kiss. His arms around me. His scent. His affection.

With my mom healing and back in Alabama and Jordan in my life, I was home.

* * *

After settling my mom into Jordan's parents' house, all I wanted to do was spend my first night back on campus with Jordan at his house. But, because bad-timing seemed to be our thing, he was hopping on a bus for Mississippi. He didn't want to leave me on my first weekend back, but I assured him I'd stay in my dorm room and order takeout until he returned. Plus, I had lots of school work to catch up on.

That night, Raquel and I threw our pillows on the floor and created a soft place to lay and catch up. We talked for a long time about what happened to my mom, and growing up in a home with an abusive stepdad. I hoped I wouldn't be such an enigma to her anymore because that had never been my intention. Now I realized, I had a good friend in her if only I let her in. She also filled me in on her family. It felt good to finally learn more about her, though I knew she was still full of surprises.

Someone knocked on our door and we both stilled, listening for whomever it was to announce themselves.

"Em." Jordan's voice carried through the door.

Raquel and I relaxed, laughing when we realized we'd both been holding our breaths.

I jumped to my feet and unlocked the deadbolt before pulling open the door.

Jordan stood there in low-hanging sweats and a blue T-shirt, which accentuated his eyes.

"I thought you left?"

"I couldn't leave without seeing you one more time," he said as he pulled me into his chest and wrapped his arms around me.

Raquel sighed behind us, making sure to exaggerate it so we could hear.

Jordan chuckled before dropping a peck on my lips. "I'll call and text. You need to do the same."

"I will."

"There's one more thing."

My brows shot up. "What?"

"Go on a date with me."

My head flinched back. "What?"

"We've never actually gone on a date and I think it'd be a good thing for us to do. You know, do what normal people do when they start dating."

My heart thumped in my chest, never so anxious for a weekend to end so I could see him again. "Okay."

"Good," he smiled. "When I get back, I'm picking you up and we're doing something fun."

I laughed, continually surprised by him.

"I'm gonna miss you," he said, before kissing me one last time, this time slow and soft and weakening my knees.

"Jealous roommate right here. Could you stop rubbing your happiness in my face?"

We both laughed as we looked to Raquel sitting amongst the mound of pillows on the floor.

"I'll talk to you later," Jordan said as his hand drifted over my cheek. He stepped back and motioned to the door as he stepped through it into the hallway. "Close this. And lock it."

I nodded, pulling the door closed slowly so I could see him right up until it clicked shut.

"I want a Grady for myself," Raquel said as I locked the deadbolt.

I turned away from the closed door and looked to her. "You sure you could handle him?"

She shook her head. "Nah, he's too hooked on you. That's for damn sure."

* * *

"When are you gonna break the news to Flip?" Raquel asked as we watched the football game on television Saturday night. "That's if Grady hasn't already rubbed it in his face."

"Flip deserves it."

Raquel's mouth dropped. "That's the meanest thing I've ever heard you say."

"He tried to keep Jordan and me apart. That's not cool."

"It's still gonna sting to know you're dating the enemy."

"You make it sound so dramatic," I laughed.

"Nope, but guys are territorial. And those two already hate each other. What's next for them? A gunfight at noon? A duel at sundown? Lightsabers?" Her voice trailed off as Flip threw a long pass down the field on TV. We waited with bated breath to see who caught it. A Mississippi player.

"Nooo," I cried.

The Mississippi player sped down the sideline with the ball under his arm to the deafening roar of the home crowd. He neared their end zone, looking ready to throw himself right into it. Out of nowhere, Jordan came barreling at him, lowering himself and throwing his arm around the player's hips, stripping the football right out of his arm as they both tumbled to the ground.

"Yessss!" I screamed, moving so close to the television it was a wonder I could see anything.

Jordan wasn't done. He jumped up and grabbed the loose ball, tucked it under his arm, and ran. I'd never seen him move so fast. The weight he'd lost made him faster and, dare I say, stealthier. Jordan's teammates blocked for him, keeping the Mississippi players at bay as he hit the fifty-yard-line…then the forty…the thirty…the twenty…the ten…Touchdown!

Raquel and I jumped around our room as Jordan spiked the ball into the end zone. Within seconds, he was encircled by his teammates jumping all over him. The camera zoomed in for a brief moment, and I could see Jordan beaming with pride from under his helmet.

Flip ran toward him, waiting for the guys to release him so he could slap his hand.

I stilled, waiting for Jordan's reaction. I saw the moment he spotted Flip. He paused then lifted his fist for Flip to tap. They separated after, the fans none the wiser to the fact that they hated each other.

They ended up winning by seven.

Raquel took off to take a shower while I watched the post-game, hoping they'd interview Jordan. They did. His helmet was off, his cheeks flushed, and his sweaty hair jutted out all over.

"Great game, Jordan," the sideline reporter greeted him with her pretty smile.

My body buzzed watching his cool demeanor as he answered her questions like the star he was always meant to be.

"What do you think was different about today's game for you?"

He smirked, and I couldn't fathom what he'd say. "Right now," he said, his eyes looking directly into the camera. "Things are going very well for me in all aspects of my life. I've got the support from my coaches and teammates, as well as my parents and my amazing girlfriend."

My entire being melted into a useless pile of goo at the sound of the word *girlfriend* out of his mouth.

"I think that carried out onto the field today," he continued.

"It did," the reporter assured him. "Thanks for taking the time, Jordan," she said.

"Thank you," he said, before she sent it back to the studio.

I sat there, long after the interview ended. I wanted to pinch myself. I wanted to be sure it was all real. Getting something you've wanted for such a long time was unlike any other feeling out there. It was surreal. And scary. But it was also…amazing.

CHAPTER TWENTY-FIVE

Grady

I couldn't fucking wait to see Emery. It had been tough being away from her, especially knowing she was alone and otherwise unprotected on campus without me there. But, we'd spoken and texted, which gave me some relief.

I climbed the stairwell until I reached her floor, unusually nervous—probably because I didn't want to mess up our first date. I'd worn a navy Henley, dark jeans, and a navy hat pulled down low—the way Emery liked it. I was going for casual but not too casual. She knew me better than anyone else, so I didn't want her to think I was trying too hard. Though I totally was.

I made my way to her door, stopping outside of it. I stared at their sign asking visitors to announce themselves. To anyone else, it seemed as though they were channeling ancient times when suitors were required to be announced. But I knew the truth behind the sign. I knew why it was imperative they didn't open the door for anyone. Why my girlfriend needed to constantly look over her shoulder. And it sucked.

"Em, it's me," I said through the door, tapping gently on it.

It took a minute, but the door opened.

My breath caught in my throat at the sight of her standing there. Her hair hung in loose curls. Her makeup was minimal but enough to tell me she wanted to look good for me. And her red strapless dress ended mid-thigh so there was still something left to the imagination. "Wow."

She smiled, looking just as nervous as I felt.

"You look hot," I said, stepping into her and cupping her cheeks with my hands. "I missed you." My lips captured hers before she could respond. The taste of her fruity lip gloss, mixed with her familiar sweet scent, blasted through my senses as I tried to get closer to her. My tongue traced the inside of her cheeks before sucking on her tongue. I eventually pulled back, breathless and hard as a damn rock. "We should probably go before we give your entire floor a show."

"You think?" she asked, just as breathless.

I glanced over her shoulder, noticing Raquel wasn't inside her room. "No audience tonight?"

She shook her head. "She had a date."

"And so do you." I held out my hand. "Shall we?"

She smiled and slipped her hand into mine. We walked slower than usual to my truck parked outside. We were in no rush. We were just enjoying being together. As we stepped outside into the early evening, I noticed her glance around, something I was beginning to realize she did out of habit. She and her mom had constantly needed to look over their shoulders. Now that threat was even more real than it had been before. And I hated that she wouldn't breathe easily until Wayne was in police custody.

I opened the passenger side of my truck and Emery hopped in. I closed her door, circled around the truck, and got in behind the wheel.

"Are you gonna tell me where we're going?" she asked.

"Nope."

She tossed back her head and laughed, and I couldn't believe how much comfort that laugh brought me. How much it had *always* brought me. Since I was eleven years old, it had been what brightened even my worst day.

Emery

I wondered if Jordan noticed me stealing glances at him as he drove off campus and through town. He looked so damn hot, and I couldn't wait to see what he had planned. I would've been lying if I said I wasn't nervous. This was Jordan. The boy I only ever dreamt would take me on a date or call me his girlfriend. *Gahhh.* I almost couldn't stand how happy I was.

"So, can we talk about that amazing play?" I asked.

"We can talk about that amazing play all-freaking-night if you want to," he laughed.

"It was so good," I gushed.

"Yeah, well, with the number of replays it got on ESPN last night and this morning, I'm hoping, like Coach said, teams have taken notice. Plays like that are the only thing that'll keep me on their radar. I'm not a quarterback, receiver, or running back. They get the headlines. I get the pain and leg injuries."

"Jordan, they'd be foolish not to give you a chance."

His eyes cut to mine. "You're biased. And have to say that because you want my body."

Laughter burst out of me.

His smile sprang to life as he focused back on the road. Five minutes later, he pulled into the parking lot of a boat rental shop on Lake Tuscaloosa. "Wait here," he said as he pushed open his door and hopped out. He circled around to my side and pulled open the door. "Ready?"

"I think so."

He took hold of my hand and helped me out of the truck before leading me around the shop to the dock behind it. A beautiful boat was tied to the dock. Tiny white lights draped from the mast to form a cone-shaped canopy. "You like?"

"It's so pretty," I said. "But do you know how to sail?"

"Um, no. That would be scary."

I laughed.

He tugged on my hand. "Come on. The captain's gonna take us out so we can watch the sun set."

My feet remained planted as I gaped at Jordan.

"What's wrong?" he asked.

"You're taking me on a boat?"

He nodded.

"Why?"

"Why?"

I nodded. "Yes, why?"

A confident smirk spread across his lips. "Because it's your perfect first date."

I laughed to myself, still amazed by how much he remembered. I let him move me to the side of the boat. I was definitely floating on cloud nine.

An older man stood by the ropes holding the boat to the dock. "Hello," he offered us a warm smile.

"Hi," we said as he bent down and untied one of the ropes.

"Come on," Jordan said to me, slipping off his shoes and leaving them on the dock before stepping onto the boat.

I slipped off my shoes and followed him on board, taking in the surroundings. It wasn't a big boat. But there was a table set up with a black tablecloth and two place settings that took up most of the back-deck area. "I can't believe you did all of this for me."

He stepped up behind me and slipped his hands around my hips, pulling me back into his chest. "I'd do a lot of things for you."

A delicious shiver rolled through me as he bent his head and pressed his lips to my neck, peppering my skin with open-mouth kisses that sent my eyes rolling into the back of my head.

"You ready to sail," our captain asked.

Jordan lifted his head, leaving my skin bereft. "You bet." He led me over to a cushioned bench seat at the back of the boat and we sat. He slipped his arm around my shoulders as our captain started the engine. The boat roared to life, quieting as we slowly pulled away from the dock and drifted toward the horizon.

There was a comfortable silence as we moved through the water. Trees lined both sides of the lake while the sun inched beneath the horizon in front of us. I breathed in Jordan's scent, something that was becoming familiar again. It wasn't the cologne he wore in high school. It was manly now. Strong. Bold. I wondered what he was thinking. Was he nervous like I was? Scared we'd mess this thing between us up?

"This is a beautiful view," I said, trying to break the silence.

"It sure is," Jordan said, though I could sense he was looking at me and not the sun.

I glanced to him. "Oh, you're just full of lines, aren't you?"

"Only the best for you."

"Seriously," I said, pulling away from his arm and turning to look at him. "Is this how you treated the other girls you dated? Sunset cruises? Corny lines?"

"First of all, my lines aren't corny."

I rolled my eyes, not even bothering with a response.

His features sobered and his voice became serious. "Em, you're not other girls."

I cocked my head, calling bullshit.

"I'm serious. With you, I can be myself. My *old* self. The one you followed around town every day. The one you never doubted would play college football. The one—who even when he was too stupid to see what was right in front of him—you hung on for the both of us. You deserve every line. Every amazing first date. Every good thing in this world."

I pulled in a much-needed deep breath. He. Was. Good. I reached up and cupped his cheeks, the same way he had held mine earlier. "The only thing I deserve…the only thing I want…is you."

"You are making this very hard," he said.

"What?"

"Being here and controlling myself."

I laughed.

"Because all I really want to do is get you alone and have you all to myself."

"We're alone," I said.

"We're in the middle of a damn lake with an audience."

Our eyes shifted to our captain, watching us in the mirror above the wheel.

"Why don't we eat," Jordan suggested, standing and pulling me to my feet.

We walked the two steps to the table and he pulled out my chair before sitting down in his. He reached under the table and removed a bag, pulling out two take-out boxes.

I laughed.

"What'd you expect?" he grinned. "Filet mignon?"

"I think it's awesome," I assured him, because I did think it was awesome. I didn't need to be wined and dined. I just wanted to be with him.

He placed one container in front of me and the other in front of him. "Go ahead," he said, nodding to my box.

I opened it and laughter burst out of me. It was a three-decker peanut butter, jelly, and fried banana sandwich. "Where did you find this?"

"It wasn't easy. I almost had to make it myself."

"I love these."

"I know. I remember."

My eyes lifted to his. There weren't enough words to convey how much it meant to me that he remembered something like that. I'd spent years thinking he'd forgotten me. Forgotten our friendship. Forgotten our kiss. Those thoughts had tortured me in more ways than one. So, to now have him remember so many small things and surprise me with them, it meant more than anything.

He smiled, as if he'd heard everything I'd been thinking.

"What do you have?" I asked, looking to his closed box.

"The same."

"You hate them."

He opened the box and picked up his sandwich. "These days I'm trying new things."

"Oh, yeah? How's that working out for you?"

"I'd say I'm doin' all right," he said, before biting into his sandwich and trying not to cringe.

I giggled as I picked up my sandwich. I could barely get my fingers around it. But that wouldn't stop me. I bit into it, groaning in pleasure. "So, good," I said with a mouthful.

He smiled, and even though I knew he hated the sandwich, he took another bite of his own. "My parents love having your mom with them," he said with a mouthful.

"Do they really or are you just being nice?"

"No, I'm serious. My mom is so occupied with your mom, she hasn't been nagging my dad."

I laughed. "It's only for a short time. My mom told me she found a gated community she liked nearby."

"My dad's gonna be disappointed."

We laughed as we ate more of our sandwiches.

"When do you think they'll find Wayne?" I asked, the thought never far from my mind.

"I wish I knew. My dad's in contact with the police in town and back in Arizona every day. They've promised to be open with him for everyone's safety."

The idea of Wayne being out there somewhere—the unknown of it all—still kept me up at night, though I didn't dare tell Jordan for fear that he'd worry too much about me.

The captain turned the boat, and I could see we were heading back to where we boarded.

"So, what do you have planned next?" I asked.

"Skinny dipping."

"Liar."

"No, I'm serious."

"Okay." I agreed.

His head shot back. "Okay?"

I nodded.

"Well, dammit. I never thought you'd say okay."

"Jordan Grady. Don't you know I'd follow you anywhere?"

He stared at me, his blue eyes studying me.

I held his gaze, waiting him out.

"Let's save skinny dipping for another night," he finally said.

I nodded, eager to find out what else he had up his sleeve.

CHAPTER TWENTY-SIX

Emery

We pulled up to Jordan's house a short while later. The last time I'd been there was the football party—the first time I'd seen him again.

He parked in the driveway and switched off the engine, turning to look at me. "You ready?"

I nodded, though I had no idea what exactly would happen inside.

"Wait there," he said, before jumping out and pulling open my door. He took my hand and helped me out.

"Is your roommate home?" I asked as we walked to the front porch hand in hand.

"Man, I hope not."

I laughed, loving how honest he always was.

We climbed the steps and Jordan unlocked the front door. A tremor of nerves shot through me as I stepped inside. We'd be all alone. In a big empty house. With his bedroom right upstairs. Was this the night? He'd said on the boat he wanted to get me alone. Was this what he meant? Was this what he wanted all along?

"So, this is my place," he said, stepping in behind me and locking the door. "I know you were here before, but with all the people, and me being a drunk asshole, you probably didn't get to check it out."

I checked out the scarce furniture and multiple TVs with video game boxes and wires stretched across the floor. It was definitely a guys' house.

"I'd ask if you wanted to play, but I know how you feel about video games." He ticked his head toward the sofa. "Come sit. I have something for you."

"What?" I asked, lowering myself to the old sofa.

"Hold on. It's a surprise." He took off for the stairs and climbed them, the old steps creaking as he disappeared.

I pulled my phone from my wristlet to check if my mom called. She hadn't. It was always a relief when she hadn't because it meant nothing was wrong. But at the same time, it left me disappointed because it meant Wayne hadn't been caught. I tucked my phone away and waited for Jordan.

After a few minutes, he returned carrying a flat box wrapped in newspaper. He sat down beside me on the sofa. The cushion dipped with his weight and the sagging cushion pulled me closer to him. "For you," he said, handing me the box.

I took it from him, and it was heavier than I thought it would be. "What is it?"

"You'll see."

I set the box down in my lap and tore away the wrapping. I lifted off the cover. A brown leather photo album sat inside. Tearing my eyes away, I glanced to Jordan who watched me intently.

"Open it."

I lifted the album, pushing the wrapping and box onto the sofa. I flipped open to the front page. Jordan's familiar handwriting had written: *It's always been you.* My heart squeezed in my chest as I glanced to him. He looked nervous but eager for me to continue. So I did, turning to the next page. My breath whooshed out of me as I stared down at the words *Year One.* A picture of Jordan and me after his peewee football game sat in the center of the page. I was eight. My hair hung in braids while Jordan's face was beet red after a tough game. It was my first time seeing him play. And I remember loving every minute of it and deciding in that moment that I'd be at every one of his games. And I was—even if I was watching online and not in person.

I flipped the page. Beneath the words *Year Two* were several pictures. Jordan and me in his backyard. At the creek. Roasting marshmallows at a campfire. Both a year older. Both having just as much fun.

My fingers traced the pictures fondly. "I remember all of these moments."

"Me too," he said, leaning in so he could look at the pictures.

"I can't believe you didn't delete these."

"You're not the only one who kept things. Some my mom had on her phone. But most of them were on mine. I couldn't delete them, Em. Even when I was so angry at you for leaving me, I couldn't erase you from my life completely." He wrapped his arm around my shoulder and pressed a kiss to the side of my head as I flipped to the next page. Then the next. Each page was a new year.

And with each year brought more pictures of all the new experiences for the two of us as we grew up together. Jordan had them all captured here. When I reached the last page, it was empty except for the word *Finally*. My eyes cut to his.

A slow smile lifted one side of his mouth as he pulled out his phone and held it up for a selfie. We both leaned in. "Finally," he said before snapping a picture.

I glanced to him as he checked out our selfie, swallowing down the nervous knot creeping up my throat. "Are you gonna show me your room?"

His eyes widened, taken aback by my boldness. "Is that what you want?"

Trying not to show my nerves, I kept my eyes confident and nodded.

Jordan stood first, reaching for my hand. I placed the album at my side and grasped hold of his hand. He pulled me up and into his chest, staring down at me. He said nothing, but his gaze spoke volumes.

He eventually moved us to the stairs and we climbed them slowly. With each step, my heartbeat accelerated. Once we reached the second floor, it was a jackhammer. Jordan moved to the first door on the right and pushed it open.

"This is nice," I said, observing his room as my thrashing heart threatened to burst out of my chest. His bed was made and the top of his dresser was empty except for a bottle of cologne.

"Were you expecting bras hanging from the bedpost?"

I shook my head. "Panties from the ceiling fan."

He laughed. "You offering?"

I laughed, slipping my hand free from his and sitting on the edge of his bed. "Maybe."

"Just so we're clear, I would not hang them from the fan."

"No?"

He shook his head. "I'd keep them in my pocket."

Laughter burst out of me, and the nerves building inside me slowly subsided.

Jordan moved closer, standing in front of me like a towering statue. "I like having you here."

"I like being here."

He sat beside me and grabbed hold of my right hand. "Em, I don't wanna screw this up."

"What?"

"You. Me." He looked around his room. "This."

"Jordan…I want to be with you. It's always been *you*."

"That's why I'm so fucking scared to mess it up."

"I'm not scared. I'm not even nervous anymore. I've waited…for *you*."

He tilted his head, heat blazing like an inferno in his eyes.

"No one has ever made me feel the way you have, Jordan. I've compared everyone to you."

"That's a lot to live up to."

I shook my head. "There's nothing to live up to. You've always been you without apology. And that's who I want."

He lifted his left hand and brushed his thumb lightly over my bottom lip. "God, I wish I was the guy you think I am."

"You *are*," I assured him, my lip tingling from his touch.

He sat there saying nothing. The silence was deafening.

Before I lost my nerve, I stood up. My knees shook as I turned so my back faced him. I glanced over my shoulder at his bewildered face. "Will you unzip me?"

He stared at me unmoving, making me reconsider my boldness.

"Jordan?" My voice cracked with the fear of rejection weighing heavily on me.

He stood up, moving slowly behind me. Instead of unzipping my dress, he pressed his chest to my back and slipped his arms around my hips, pressing a trail of open-mouthed kisses from my neck to my shoulder. A shudder rushed through me as my head dropped back, resting against him as he continued his pursuit on the other side.

"If this is you messing up," I breathed. "I never want you to stop."

He chuckled against my neck and a shiver skated over my skin. He moved his arms, his hands drifting slowly up my back. His fingers took hold of my zipper. He tugged it down an inch, following the movement with a kiss to the revealed skin. He pulled it down another inch, and his lips were there, kissing my back. Another inch and he needed to bend so his mouth could follow. Finally, the zipper stopped, having no more teeth to pull it any lower. Jordan stood up, and paused.

"It's okay," I whispered.

He released my dress. It pooled at my feet, leaving me in nothing but a black thong. Instinctively, I crossed my arms over my bare breasts even though Jordan was still behind me. As eager as I was for this next step with him, being mostly naked in front of anyone was new to me.

His hands slipped down to my hips. I quivered under his touch as his fingers moved up and down slowly as his mouth found my ear. He nibbled his way around the outer lobe before he added his tongue. Goosebumps erupted over my skin. I lifted my arms and wrapped them around his neck, needing to hold on to something to steady my trembling legs. His hands slipped around to my bare stomach as he moved to my other ear. The stimulation was almost too much. I'd never been this vulnerable. This turned on. I needed to kiss him. I needed to feel him. I was about to turn in his arms when his hands ventured up my stomach.

I pulled in a sharp breath when his hands slowly coasted over my breasts. My breaths became shallow. The pulsing between my thighs was intense. "Oh, God."

His mouth drifted down my neck as his hands began to kneed my breasts, his thumbs tracing my nipples. When I didn't think I was going to be able to take anymore, he tugged on my nipple, sending tremors shooting between my thighs. My knees nearly buckled. He did it again. I couldn't take anymore. The tremors between my legs pulsed in rhythmic beats. "Jordan," I whimpered.

"Em," he said between kisses to my shoulder. "You feel so good."

"Bed," I said, incapable of a coherent sentence.

He twisted me in his arms and his lips crashed down on mine. I wasn't the only one having difficulty controlling myself. His tongue dipped inside my mouth, entangling with mine, fighting for control. He walked us back toward the bed. When the backs of my knees hit the bed, he picked me up and lowered me down in the center. He pulled back and kneeled over me. It was the first time he was seeing me virtually naked and his eyes lit up as they wandered over me.

I pushed myself up onto my elbows and stared back, wondering what he was thinking. He'd seen me at all my awkward stages, but he'd never seen me like this.

"You're a dream come true," he said, before reaching behind his neck and pulling his shirt over his head.

My cheeks pulsed with heat, undoubtedly reddening as he stood. I watched him strip down to his boxers then step toward the bed.

"Wait."

His eyes narrowed.

I swallowed down hard. "Take off your boxers."

A slow cocky grin slid across his lips before he unabashedly pushed his boxers down his legs.

I tried not to stare, but I'd never seen a naked guy before. Sure, I'd seen them online, but not like this. Not right in front of me. Not Jordan. And I knew, by the looks of…*it*, he was ready if I was. I stared at him. He stared back. With bated breath, I nodded slightly, giving him the okay.

Jordan didn't hesitate, moving forward and climbing on top of me. I lay back, slipping my arms around his hips as he covered me with his naked body. He braced his weight on his elbows beside my head and gazed down at me. "If this is as far as we go tonight, it would still be perfect."

"For who?" I asked, incredulously.

"I told you I don't want to ruin this, Em. And sleeping together on the first date is a surefire way to do that."

"Says who?"

"Anyone who's done it."

"But they're not you and me. And they haven't waited almost their entire life to have you look at them the way you're looking at me right now. So, I say we make up our own rules. And we do what feels right for us."

He bent his head and kissed me slowly, giving me what I wanted.

My hands drifted up his back, his tight muscles forming dips and valleys under his smooth skin. His lower body relaxed on top of me, and my thong's single strip of material didn't shield me from the hard length of him pressing between us.

My fingertips skated down his back, sliding over the dip beneath his spine and over his ass. My fingernails dug into his skin as his mouth continued to torture me slowly. I wanted to feel him between my legs. I wanted to feel him inside of me. I shifted my hips, trying to get closer. The head of his penis brushed me. *Holy. Hell.* I shifted again, trying to hit the same spot. My eyes rolled back as the friction sent zingers to my core.

Both of us were panting hard when Jordan pulled back from my mouth. "Em, I'm having a really hard time controlling myself right now, and you shifting your ass and trying to rub up on my dick is sending me pretty close to the edge."

The matter-of-fact way he said it made my belly ripple.

"And, while that's not always a bad thing," he continued. "Tonight, I wanna make this good for you."

"It already *is* good," I assured him.

"Yeah, well, just because you're stroking my ego right now, doesn't mean I want it over in five minutes."

I nodded again, realizing he wasn't upset, more frustrated he couldn't control himself.

"Now you need to promise me, for the next few minutes, you're not going to touch me."

"Okay."

"I don't believe you." He reached down, grabbed my wrists, and pinned my arms above my head.

I couldn't move. And I liked it. More than I ever thought I would. My chest rose and fell, my body buzzing with need.

Jordan released my wrists.

I didn't dare move.

"There are a million things I want to do with you," he said, all raspy and sexy. "And having you spread out like this is testing my resolve—"

"Jordan, I want you inside of me," I blurted, unable to stop my horniness from speaking for me.

He closed his eyes, as if in pain.

But why? I'd told him what I wanted. I didn't want there to be any confusion. Was that wrong?

He opened his eyes. "That's the hottest thing anyone's ever said to me."

Nervous laughter rushed out of me.

He gazed down at me, probably realizing my boldness came from never having felt such intense sensations happening to my body at one time. He reached into his nightstand and grabbed a small package. I didn't peek to see if he had a huge stash. This was about him and me. No one who'd come before mattered now. He tore open the packet then reached down, rolling the condom on. He braced himself once again, hovering over me. "I—"

"Stop talking." I lowered my arms and pulled his mouth down to mine, kissing him the way I wanted to be kissed. My tongue pushed inside his mouth. I was in control now, and my tongue was hell-bent on consuming him.

With our tongues melded together, Jordan reached down and pulled my thong off my legs. Now there was nothing between us. Nothing stopping us from going further. He reached down and dragged his thumb over my wet folds. My eyes pinched shut. Then he hit my clit. I gasped, the sensations overpowering. He kept at it, stroking relentlessly with the pad of his thumb. Circling. Stroking. Circling. Stroking. *God.* Glorious throbbing beat like a bass drum between my legs. I focused on the eruption inevitably awaiting me. But all too soon, Jordan withdrew his hand.

He pulled back from my mouth and stared down at me. "Are you sure about this, Em?"

"Yes," I breathed.

He reached down and positioned himself between my legs, guiding the head of his penis up and down my wet skin. I was ready for him. And if his thumb was any indication of the pleasure awaiting me, I was all in.

I expected him to thrust inside me. To push until the pain I'd heard about subsided. But he didn't. He continued moving his erection over me. Back and forth. Circling my clit. Then back and forth again. Was he purposely teasing me? Or was he making sure I was ready?

My panting must have clued him that I was turned on beyond reason because he pushed the head of his penis inside me an inch. "How's this?" he asked.

"Keep going," I said, my eyes locked on his.

He pushed in a little more. "Still good?"

"Stop talking and do it," I said.

He kept his eyes on mine and pushed the rest of the way inside me. Thanks to the wetness he created, he slid right in. His eyes never wavered from mine as he stretched me wide. "I love being this close to you."

His words and the feel of him inside me proved too much. Tears glazed my eyes.

"Am I hurting you?"

I shook my head, unable to articulate what I was feeling. I'd never imagined he and I could actually physically be one. But in that moment, with him inside of me, I felt like we were. Wild emotions rocked through me, happiness trumping them all.

Jordan pulled out slowly and pushed back inside me. I was getting used to the feel of him. It didn't hurt like I'd heard it would. It felt right. He pulled back again and pushed inside me, his thrusting gaining a slow and steady rhythm. He lowered his mouth to mine and kissed me slowly as he continued to move inside of me. He somehow kept himself balanced as he reached one hand down between us and moved his thumb over my clit. A fluttering sensation started up. Then tingling. And tremors. The fact that he was stretching me wide, made the sensations more intense. The throbbing became harder. Something was building inside me. Something was coiling up and ready to bubble over.

"Jordan," I whimpered.

"Just relax and let it happen," he said, burying his face in the crook of my neck. His thrusting became faster and his thumb stroked harder.

I closed my eyes and let myself be in the moment. But it was difficult to stop images of Jordan and me at all stages of our lives from flashing through my mind. All the hopes that he would one day want me flooded my body as intensely as the throbbing between my thighs.

He moved his thumb around, circling my clit until my body clenched around him and erupted in a rush of sensations. My body quaked, humming with the glorious after-tremors.

Jordan didn't let up. He thrust harder and deeper until he stilled, a growl rumbling out of him. He lowered down on top of me as I wrapped my arms tighter around him. He stayed inside me, pulsing until we'd both come back down to Earth.

"Is it always like that?" I whispered.

"God, no." He pulled away from my neck so he could see me, his cheeks flushed and his face beaded with sweat. "I've never felt anything like that."

"Don't just say that."

"Em, you waited for me. That alone made it amazing. Are you hurting?"

"Only in the best possible way," I said.

He leaned down and kissed me hard. "Keep stroking my ego, baby."

I snorted.

He pulled out of me slowly.

A sense of loss passed over me as Jordan rolled off the bed. He removed the condom and discarded it in a trash bin. "Be right back." He opened his door and padded down the hallway. He returned a minute later, locking the door behind him and crawling back onto the bed with a wash cloth. "This might be a little cool." He reached between my legs and ran the damp cloth along my folds. My head dropped back as he did, not having any idea what he was doing until he stood and I could see a hint of blood on the cloth.

I cringed. "Sorry."

He folded the cloth and tossed it into the trash bin. "Nothing to be sorry about." He returned to the side of the bed. "Let's snuggle."

I smiled as I moved under the sheets.

Jordan crawled in and pulled me into him, fitting me into the hard planes of his chest. "Thank you, Em."

My brows lifted. "For what?"

"Letting me be your first."

It took everything in me not to add, 'And hopefully my last.'

CHAPTER TWENTY-SEVEN

Emery

I awoke wrapped in Jordan's soft sheets as sunlight peeked through his curtains. The previous night rivaled the most amazing dream. I rolled over, only to find an empty spot beside me. I sat up, hugging the sheets to me and listening for the shower down the hallway or movement downstairs. There was nothing.

I wondered if anything would change in the light of day. Had the cloak of darkness given me a boldness I'd no longer possess? Would things between us be awkward now that we had to navigate a relationship?

The doorknob suddenly rattled.

I stilled.

For the first time since being with Jordan, an anxious feeling clutched my chest. Thoughts of Wayne bombarded me. He'd disappeared from my mind while in Jordan's arms.

Damn him.

The door pushed in and I unconsciously crept back toward the headboard, as if that would somehow protect me.

Jordan maneuvered himself inside the room, balancing two coffees in one hand and a plate of food in the other.

Air punched out of my lungs. I scrambled off the bed with the sheet wrapped around me to help him. As my nerves slowly subsided, I took one of the coffees from him. "What are you doing?"

"I brought breakfast."

"I can see that, but why didn't you wake me?"

"You were sleeping. I didn't want to stop your dreams."

I stared back at him. Didn't he get that he *was* my dream? Always had been. Always would be. *Gahhhh*. I was so far gone it would be impossible to return. That, I was sure of. "Thank you."

He sat down on the bed and I cozied up next to him against the headboard. We drank coffee and picked at the dish of fruit he brought up.

"I've got class in about an hour."

He nodded. "I know. I'm gonna drive you back to your dorm and walk you to class."

"I appreciate that, but you've got your own classes and football to worry about. It's broad daylight with thousands of people around. I'm not nervous. I'll be okay."

"I know. But maybe I want to spend time with you. Do things for you. Be seen with your hot self."

I rolled my eyes.

"What? I'm serious."

"Seriously crazy."

"Never claimed not to be. But now I'm crazy about you. So deal, woman."

I shook my head. This sudden switch in our relationship was going to take time to get used to. Being in the dark, with our bodies wrapped around one another was one thing. But in the light of day, with all the outside factors at play, I needed to figure out how we worked. How to act around him. How to be the new us.

Forty minutes later, Jordan waited in my dorm room to take me to class. He'd showered at his house and changed into basketball shorts and a T-shirt with a hat pulled down low. I threw on jeans and a T-shirt, slipped on my flip-flops, and tried to twist the strap of my bag across me, but Jordan grabbed it from me.

The walk across campus with Jordan was…different. Lots of guys held out their fists for him to bump and multiple girls stared as we passed by. But regardless of their looks, he kept my hand in his and his eyes on me.

"Grady," a girl called.

He stopped, holding me back with him.

A beautiful blonde stopped in front of us. She looked questioningly to him, like he should know what she was thinking.

"Em, this is Sabrina," he said with a grin, alleviating any fears I may have had that she was an angry ex or one-night-stand. "Sabrina, this is Em."

"Nice to finally meet you," Sabrina said with a smile. "Anyone who can put up with his shenanigans is a good person in my book."

I laughed. "Yeah, someone's got to do it. And since I've known him since he was eleven, I think I'm up for the challenge."

Sabrina laughed. "Challenge is definitely the word I'd use for him."

"Hey, I'm right here, ladies. And I've yet to hear anything about my glowing personality or killer body."

Sabrina and I rolled our eyes, both pretending not to be amused by him.

"And for the record," Sabrina said to him. "We were friends before the hot body."

Jordan threw his head back and howled in a way I'd never heard him do before. "Did you hear her, Em? Not only did she admit we're friends, she also said I have a hot body. All in the same sentence. I never thought I see the day."

Sabrina pointed right into his chest. "If you tell anyone, I will kill you."

"Em's my witness," Jordan said.

Sabrina grinned and shook her head. Then she said to me, "When he's not around, we'll have to grab a coffee and you can fill me in on what you see in him."

I nodded. "That would be nice."

Sabrina walked away without so much as a backward glance.

"*She* was interesting," I said, unsure what to make of their exchange.

Jordan started walking again. "Yeah, she wants to hate me, but she just can't seem to do it."

"Why?"

He shrugged. "I gave her roommate shit when I first met her, so she wanted to hate me for that. But then she got to know me, and my uncle helped her and her hockey player boyfriend with some legal stuff."

"So, she has a boyfriend?" I said, trying to hide the fact that the information brought me relief.

"Yeah. He plays professional hockey now. She won't be around here long. She'll follow him up north, no doubt."

"Why weren't you nice to her friend?"

I shrugged.

"No, tell me."

His lips twisted as he contemplated whether he should. "I hated the world after you disappeared. I didn't trust people."

My stomach clenched uncomfortably at his words. I hated that I'd hurt him.

"And I sure as hell didn't want to stand by and watch a weak female put up with mistreatment—like you had to do for your mom's sake. So, when I first saw Finlay—that's Sabrina's friend—I knew she needed to toughen up if she was gonna put up with a bunch of rowdy football players. So, I gave her shit until she gave it back. I guess I just saw you in her. And I wanted her to stand up for herself."

"You don't think I stood up for myself?" I asked, disappointed he viewed me that way.

He stopped us and tunneled both hands in my hair so his nose was almost touching mine. "I think you're one of the strongest people I know. The fact that you lived that way with Wayne and still smiled every day, showed how strong you really are. Do I wish we could have stood up to him and gotten him out of your house? Hell yes. But we were kids. And it was something we couldn't do."

I nodded, his words stealing my breath away and silencing my fears.

"Now," he said, pulling back a little. "Let me walk my girlfriend to class so everyone on this campus can see me with her."

I laughed. "You really are crazy."

"And you love it, baby."

* * *

Jordan stood outside my building after class ended, looking all hot and protective.

I greeted him with a smile. "You take your bodyguard duties very seriously, don't you?"

"If anyone's gonna be guarding your body, it's me." He dropped a kiss on the top of my head as he swung his arm over my shoulders and walked me back toward my dorm.

"That line's never gonna get old for you, huh?"

"Not likely."

We ended up back at my dorm a few minutes later. "Let me walk you upstairs," Jordan said, outside the front door.

"I'm fine." I patted his chest gently as I pulled the strap of my bag over his head. "Now, hurry up. You don't want to be late for your class."

"I don't care about that."

I scanned my ID card beside the door. It buzzed and the door unlocked. I pulled it open. "Have fun," I said.

"Yeah." Jordan laughed before turning and jogging away. He was definitely going to be late.

I closed the front door behind me and climbed the steps to my floor. I walked down my hallway and stopped outside my room. I typed in the passcode on my door. I must've missed a number because it didn't unlock. I tried again, this time making sure to press each number slowly and accurately. The door unlocked. I reached for the handle.

"Emery?"

I spun around with my pulse ricocheting off my chest. Flip stood there.

"How long have you been standing there?" I asked, almost unable to speak.

Flip shrugged. "How's it going?"

I stared at him with anger flaring inside me. Not only had he scared me half to death, but he also set up Jordan. And that was not okay. "That's what you want to say to me?"

His brows dipped. "What?"

"The fight with Jordan. I heard his side."

A harsh, humorless laugh escaped him as he crossed his arms. "So, let me guess? You believe him?"

"Yup. Because he's never lied to me."

"He's in love with you, Emery. He hasn't been lying about *that*?"

"Denial and lying are two different things. What you did was lie. You skewed it so the story worked in your favor. And the sucky thing about it? I believed *you*. I didn't want to even hear his side."

He looked down.

"I was wrong to believe you. And I told Jordan that."

He glanced up at me, like he wanted to say something, but I wasn't finished yet.

"You know, it really sucks because you were my first friend here. I thought you'd be in my life for the next four years. But *you* messed that up. For no reason."

He still said nothing.

"I'm not here to lecture you, but just so you don't mess it up with the next girl you befriend you need to know something. A real friend wants you to be happy. They don't try to sabotage your happiness." I twisted the knob on my door and left Flip in the hallway as I walked into my room.

CHAPTER TWENTY-EIGHT

Grady

The home crowd filled the stadium with a roar you didn't get in any other college football stadium. Our fans were crazy about their football. And we loved it. We thrived on their cheers and we worked our asses off when we knew we'd disappointed them.

For the first time in four years, Em stood in the front row beside my dad with my number painted in white on her cheeks. I loved knowing Em was there for me and only me.

I hadn't spoken to my dick of a QB since I'd clocked his ass. Sure, he tried to celebrate my touchdown the previous week, but tapping his fist was only for show. Those potential teams—and everyone else watching at home—needed to know I was a team player. They needed to see nothing but greatness from me. Unfortunately, after last week's amazing display, I wasn't sure I could top it. So, I went into this game ready to give it one-hundred-and-ten percent effort. No one could fault me for that.

From the first snap, I was on fire. Block after block felt effortless for me. The guys and I were in sync on the field. The receivers were always right where they needed to be to catch passes. Even Flip could do no wrong when it came to his passes.

By the half, we were winning by twenty-one.

The team and I ran back out to the sideline after halftime. I glanced to my dad and Em, expecting them to be cheering with the rest of the fans, but they weren't. They were engrossed in a conversation with a man who stood in the aisle. I tried to discern who he was, but I didn't recognize him. Having no time to figure it out, I grabbed my helmet and got my ass back out on the field.

We scored again on third and fifteen, this time due to a nice hand-off to Hayes, our sophomore running back. It was good to see the younger guys getting some play and making names for themselves. As I ran off the field after the touchdown, I glanced to the stands. My dad and Em were cheering us on, and the man they'd been speaking to had disappeared.

We won again by a landslide and Flip got all the attention after the game. I jogged over to my dad and Em before heading to the locker room.

"Hey."

"Great game," Em gushed.

"Nice work out there, Jordan," my dad said.

"Thanks."

"Want to get some dinner?" my dad asked.

"Sure. I'll meet you and Em by the locker room in about twenty minutes."

He nodded and Em smiled, like she was bursting to say more.

I cocked my head in question and she just smiled.

What could I say? The crazy girl loved me.

* * *

"You guys better spill it," I said, my eyes moving between Em beside me and my dad across the table. "You've been acting weird since we left the stadium."

"Your dad has some news," Em said.

I looked to my dad for an explanation.

He sipped his drink as I waited anxiously. "An agent approached me at the game," he said.

"An agent?"

My dad nodded. "He wanted to know if you were going to the pro combine this year. I didn't know what to say to him. You never mentioned it."

My gut clenched. I had only told Em that Coach thought I might have a shot at the pros.

"Emery told me what your coach told you," my dad said. "She said you've been considering it."

"I seriously didn't think it would really happen. So why get my hopes up? But I've been having a hell of a season. And I'm starting to think I could actually make it."

"He said he's had his eye on you for a while," Em added excitedly.

"He has?"

My dad nodded. "It seems so. He's pretty interested in getting you ready for the combine and then representing you when you show what you can really do."

"Isn't that awesome?" Em asked, noticing the shock on my face.

"He said on the surface you may not necessarily be a first-round pick," my dad added. "But he believes you could be a sleeper pick for some of these teams."

"You know I can't take anything from him. Or commit, verbal or written," I said.

"All he wanted to know was if you wanted to play professional football," he said.

"And if I do?"

"He'll be in touch after the season," my dad said.

Holy shit.

* * *

I stood at the bar waiting for the beers and sodas I'd ordered. It was quieter than normal since it was Sunday night. I glanced over my shoulder to the high-top table where Em laughed with Sabrina and her boyfriend Crosby. I dropped my cash on the bar as the bartender placed my drinks down. I grabbed two in each hand and maneuvered through the scattered people milling around.

"What'd I miss?" I asked, sitting in the stool beside Em as I slid the beers onto the table in front of Sabrina and Crosby and the sodas in front of Em and me.

"Just telling Emery horror stories about you," Sabrina admitted.

"Are you serious?" I asked Sabrina but looked to Crosby for confirmation.

The traitor shrugged.

I reached over and cupped Em's ears. "Earmuffs."

She laughed and shook off my hands. "She's not saying anything that's gonna scare me off."

"Damn straight she's not," I said. "You're not going anywhere."

Em smiled, and it was lame to admit, but that smile did weird things to me.

I looked away before I did something crazy like make out with her right there in front of everyone. Sabrina stared at me, her eyes narrowing in that who-the-hell-are-you and what-have-you-done-with-Grady way.

"So, how's your team look?" I asked Crosby, ignoring Sabrina's unspoken questions.

"I think we've got potential," he said, never being one to say much.

I could tell he was kinda pissed Sabrina dragged him out with us. They barely got to see each other. I'm sure he had other plans in mind for them. But Sabrina had insisted we go out because she wanted to get to know Em.

"You guys are doing well," he added.

"Yeah. We've got a douchebag for a QB, but the rest of the team is okay."

"Yeah," Crosby scoffed. "I saw my fair share of douchebags last year."

I nodded, knowing he had a rough time once he transferred to Alabama. The hockey team made his time on the team hell. But he turned the tables on them, flipping them the proverbial bird by getting drafted to the pros.

"You thinking of going pro next year?" he asked.

I shrugged, knowing better than to talk about the agent with anyone—other than Em and my dad.

"Any team would be lucky to have him," Em said.

Sabrina laughed. "I'm not sure they'll think *that* until they get to know him."

"Am I that difficult?" I asked.

The girls answered at the same time. "Yes."

We laughed, and for once in a long time, it felt nice to have friends.

"I'll be right back," Em said to me.

I leaned over and dropped a peck on her lips. "If any guys try to talk to you, tell them you're taken. Got it?"

She laughed.

"I'm serious." I flexed my right arm and eyed my muscle. "Show them the guns."

"Oh my God." She rolled her eyes and hurried off to the bathroom.

"Just when I thought you changed," Sabrina said.

I turned back to her.

Her eyes riveted between mine. "Actually…lame comments aside…you have changed."

"Em brings out the best in me."

"And Sabrina brings out the horny side in me," Crosby said, wrapping his tattoo-sleeved arm around her and pulling her into his side.

She giggled. "Stop. You said you could wait."

"I lied." Crosby slid off his stool and said, "Dude, I need to get my girl alone before I head back. You understand, right?"

Sabrina looked just as eager to be alone with him.

"Yeah. Go. It was nice hanging with you guys."

He bumped my fist. "Later."

Sabrina unexpectedly wrapped her arms around me and leaned into my ear. "She's a keeper."

"Tell me something I don't know," I said as she stepped back from me.

Crosby wrapped his arm around Sabrina and led her out of the bar.

Em returned a couple minutes later. She looked at the empty table. "Where'd they go?"

"I think she got what she came for."

Her nose scrunched. "What's that mean?"

"I think she just wanted to see me happy."

Her bottom lip jutted out. "So, she was looking out for you?"

"I guess she was."

She walked in between my knees and slipped her arms around my neck. "So, did she approve of me?"

"Yup."

"And if she didn't?"

I leaned in and kissed her. "Wouldn't matter."

She smiled.

CHAPTER TWENTY-NINE

Emery

I'd finished getting dressed in black skinny jeans and a fuchsia scoop-neck shirt, going for a more casual look. I had no idea where Jordan planned to take me. It had been a week since our first real date, and I wondered if he'd try to top such a special night.

I'd run to the restroom and was heading back to my room to fix my makeup. My heartbeat sped—a normal occurrence when I knew we'd be alone together. And after the amazing first week we'd had, I didn't think things could go any better.

The bass from a radio down the hall made it impossible to hear my own thoughts as I tapped the passcode into the keypad on my door and pushed it open.

The moment I stepped into my room, a cold shiver rushed up my spine and the door closed behind me.

Wayne stood in my room.

I spun back around and grabbed the door knob, but he was too fast, knocking me out of the way as he blocked the door with his body. "I just want to talk," he said.

"Not a good idea, Wayne," I said, my voice cracking and my hands shaking as I backed up into my room, locking my eyes on him.

"I'd say letting your mother drain our bank accounts and not calling to tell me where you'd gone warrants a conversation," he said, his face pale and cheeks gaunt.

Visions of what he'd done to my mother stung my eyes with tears. "The police are looking for you."

"Haven't found me yet," he said moving toward me.

"How did you find me?" I asked, back-stepping until I hit my bed.

"Wasn't too hard to figure out where you both went when you left the hospital together."

"What do you want?"

"What I'm owed."

My stomach lurched as I bolted toward the door, knowing if I didn't act quickly, he'd catch me. But he was at the door as fast as me, caging me in.

A cold gut-wrenching fear grasped hold of me.

My mother said she knew her time had come. Now I understood what she meant. Hiding for four years always made it a possibility. But this was the reality.

"Help!" I screamed, hoping someone would hear me.

Wayne covered my mouth, stealing away my breath. "Your mother fought me well." The smell of alcohol on his breath terrified me. He was rational when he was sober. He was a monster when he was drunk.

My eyes shifted to my phone on the desk. If I could just get to it. If I could just call for help.

"Scream again and I will hurt you," he warned.

The sinking feeling in the pit of my stomach told me I wasn't getting out of this unscathed.

He slowly removed his hand from my mouth, gauging my next move.

"She loved you, Wayne," I said, unable to hide the quaking in my voice. "You just never loved her back."

His hand came out of nowhere, slapping me across the face.

The sting elicited a pool of tears in my eyes.

"I loved her," he snarled. "I loved both of you."

Tears trailed down my throbbing cheek. "You don't hurt the people you love. And you hurt her repeatedly."

"She left me with nothing. I've got nothing left."

"What do you want? Money? Is that why you hurt her?"

He said nothing.

"If you could stay sober, you'd be able to hold down a job. You could make your own money."

Still, he said nothing.

So, I kept talking. Talking so he wouldn't hurt me. Talking so he would sober up. Talking so help could show up. "But what I really think you need is help, Wayne. Get help."

My words sparked a rage in his eyes. A rage I'd never seen directed at me before. "*I* need help?" His hands dropped to my shoulders and he slammed me against the door, my head bouncing off it.

I gasped as the wind was sucked out of me and I slipped down to the floor with a thud.

Wayne stared down at me.

Had something I said resonated with him?

Was he having a change of heart?

Did he feel regret?

The glazed look in his eyes told me he was too far gone for any of that. I was transported to my youth. But now I was in my mother's place.

Oh, hell no.

I jumped to my feet, frantically grabbing for the first thing I could get my hand on to fight him off. I grasped the back of the wooden desk chair, pulling it in front of me to protect me from him.

He grabbed the chair and yanked it free from my hands.

I had nothing to protect me but my bare hands. And for the first time in my life, I was ready to use them. Ready to inflict pain on the man who tried to rid this world of the woman I loved most.

The click of the door opening sent Wayne's head twisting over his shoulder.

Jordan stepped into the room with a huge smile on his face. Everything in his face changed as his eyes jumped between Wayne grasping the chair and me looking terrified. Jordan flew forward, his fists connecting with Wayne's face until he brought him to the ground. Jordan wailed on him. First a right hook, then a left. They came fast and furious and difficult to discern. Wayne tried to fight back, but Jordan was too strong. Too angry. Too lethal.

I ran to my phone. My hands shook as I dialed 9-1-1. I lifted the phone to my ear while watching Jordan's relentless pursuit to exact revenge. Wayne wasn't fighting back; he was covering his face. Blood had splattered. Wayne's blood. I didn't want Jordan to go easy on the man who'd hurt my mother, but I hated the rage in his eyes that Wayne brought out of him. This was the culmination of years of hatred. This was retribution for what Wayne had done to us.

"We need help," I explained to the operator, rattling off our location and what was happening in more of a scream than a composed response. She wanted me to stay on the line, but I needed to make Jordan stop. Wayne no longer covered his face. He lay unmoving.

Had he passed out?

Been knocked out?

"Jordan, stop!" I yelled.

He didn't. His fists had minds of their own.

"Jordan, stop! He's unconscious."

Jordan finally stopped, his head shaking slightly as if fighting off the rage jockeying for control of his brain. He straightened up, his eyes never wavering from Wayne on the floor.

"Is he breathing?" I asked.

"Unfortunately," Jordan said as he moved to me, wrapping his arms around me but never taking his eyes off Wayne. "When I walked in here…" he began.

"I know."

"I was so fucking scared."

"I know."

He looked to me. Blood stained his face and shirt. "Did he touch you?"

"He slapped and shoved me. But that was it."

His gaze dropped, looking me over. "Promise me nothing else happened."

"I promise."

He tugged me back against his chest and held me so tightly I could barely breathe. "I saw red. I saw what he did to your mom. I knew what he did to her over the years. What you had to see. I wanted to hurt him. I wanted him dead."

"We're okay. The police are on their way. He'll get what he's got coming."

Footsteps in the hallway drew our attention to the door. Jordan hadn't closed it when he walked in on Wayne and me, so two police officers entered the room with hands on the guns in their hip holsters. They spotted Wayne on the floor, unconscious.

"He armed?" the tall officer in front asked.

"I don't know," I said.

He moved toward Wayne, lowering to the floor. He pinched Wayne's wrist, feeling for a pulse.

"What happened?" the shorter officer standing behind him asked, his eyes on Jordan's bloody fists and blood-splattered face and shirt.

"Wayne attacked me," I explained. "Jordan showed up and protected me."

"You know the guy?" the officer at Wayne's side asked as he searched for a weapon on Wayne.

"He was my stepfather."

"Her *abusive* stepfather," Jordan growled through clenched teeth.

"There's a warrant out for his arrest," I explained.

"Did you invite him here?" the short one asked as he assessed my room.

"What the fuck?" Jordan released me and straightened himself defensively. "Of course she didn't. The lunatic beat up her mother and put her in the hospital. He must've followed Emery here after she left the hospital."

"He did," I said. "He pretty much told me that's how he found me."

"Are you hurt?" the shorter officer asked me.

I wrapped my arms around myself. "He slapped me…pushed me around. But mostly, I'm a little shaken up."

"He tried to kill her mother. Left her for dead," Jordan reiterated.

"Did he attack *you?*" the kneeling officer asked Jordan.

Jordan shook his head. "He didn't have time. As soon as I found him here, I pounced."

"That's when I called 9-1-1," I said.

EMTs walked through the door with a gurney, instantly attending to Wayne, all bloody and battered. We watched as they waved something under his nose. It took no more than a couple seconds and he stirred.

My body stiffened. Jordan held me, tucking me into his chest.

Wayne's eyes shot around the room, ultimately landing on Jordan. "He attacked me," Wayne said, low and menacing.

"What were you doing here?" one of the officers asked Wayne.

"Where am I?" Wayne asked, his eyes flashing around my room, as if he hadn't come to my room on his own accord.

I could feel Jordan tense. "Don't," I whispered, holding on tightly and trying to help reel in his anger.

"He's full of shit," Jordan growled.

The shorter officer, aware that Jordan could snap at any moment and attack Wayne again, moved between us and Wayne. "Don't make me cuff you," he warned Jordan.

"You better be cuffing *him*," Jordan spat.

"You don't need to tell us how to do our jobs," the officer said.

I pulled back from Jordan, holding my hands to his chest. "Jordan. They're here now. It's over."

The officer moved to Wayne. His partner already stood at Wayne's side as the EMTs transferred him onto the gurney. He groaned, and I hoped he had broken ribs like he'd given my mother. The shorter officer handcuffed Wayne to the gurney before the EMTs wheeled him to the door.

"Hope you get everything you deserve, you bastard!" Jordan called to Wayne as they disappeared into the hallway.

The taller officer walked over to us as the shorter one followed Wayne out. He pressed his hand to Jordan's chest a little harder than probably necessary. "You, my friend, need to calm down. Whether or not there's a warrant out for his arrest or not, you're the one with blood on your hands. You'll be lucky if he doesn't press charges."

"Fuck you."

"*Jordan,*" I admonished.

"He attacked my girl *and* her mom. You have no idea what I'd be capable of if he shows up here again."

The officer shook his head. "Comments like that don't make you look as innocent as you're claiming. Now I need to take you to the station—and you can react the way I think you're gonna react—"

"I did nothing wrong," Jordan argued.

"You attacked an unarmed man, beating him until he was unconscious. We have laws that say you can't do that," the officer explained.

"I want to give my statement," I said. "Jordan did nothing wrong."

"Ma'am. He can't go around beating someone to a pulp. No matter what this guy did. This is gonna take some time." He pulled his cuffs off his belt and looked to Jordan. "Make this easy on yourself. Don't give those students in the hallway with their cell phones out something that goes viral. Come to the station willingly so I can take your statement and get you back to your girlfriend who seems to have had a pretty rough night." The officer looked to me. "Call a lawyer for him. There's no doubt in my mind that that guy's going to play the victim and press charges."

"Call my uncle," Jordan said.

I nodded, knowing his uncle Cal was a damn good lawyer. I turned to the officer. "I assure you the police in multiple states have been looking for Wayne. He's a bad man. No matter what he says. He's a violent drunk who my mom finally had the courage to leave." Tears began to well up in my eyes. "We changed our names and moved away four years ago, but he tracked us down. We've suffered enough because of him."

The officer nodded, attaching his cuffs to his belt and taking Jordan's arm to move him to the door.

Jordan resisted, turning to me and cupping my cheeks. "Call your mom. Tell her the good news."

I nodded, my eyes now filled with tears.

"We're good," he assured me. "No matter what happens, we're still happening, baby."

I tried to stay strong for him, smiling through my tears as the officer led him away from me and out of my room. But the vision of him being taken away—and the knowledge that it was because of me—crushed every part of my heart.

CHAPTER THIRTY

Emery

I sat on the edge of my bed with my phone to my ear and my hand shaking wildly. I'd called Jordan's uncle Cal who was on his way to the police station. And now I was trying to reach my mom.

"Emery?" my mom answered.

"Hi, Mama. How are you?"

"Feeling stronger every day."

I wanted to smile, but every part of me trembled with fear for Jordan. "Are the Gradys there?"

"They're out back having dinner."

"Listen, Mama. I've got something to tell you."

She went silent.

"Wayne showed up here."

"What?" Fear filled her voice. "Are you okay?"

"Yeah. Jordan stopped him. He stopped him, Mama. And the police came and took Wayne away. You're safe now."

"Thank God. Where's Jordan?"

I steadied my voice, not wanting to worry her, though I was terrified myself. "He's at the police station."

"Giving a statement?"

"Kind of."

"Emery?"

"They took him to the station for attacking Wayne."

"Did you call Cal?"

"Just got off the phone with him. He's on his way to the station."

She was silent. "I wish he wasn't brought into our mess."

"He wants to be in our mess. He told me."

"He's such a good boy," my mother said.

"He is."

"What am I gonna tell his parents?" she asked.

"Just tell them the truth. And tell them Cal is on his way there. He's probably calling them as we speak."

A silent moment passed between us. I wondered if she was able to breathe easily knowing Wayne was in custody. Knowing she wouldn't need to hide anymore. Knowing she wouldn't need to constantly look over her shoulder.

"How do you feel?" I asked.

"Is it wrong to say I feel better?"

"Of course not…Listen, I've gotta go, Mama. I want to be at the police station when Jordan's released."

"Okay, honey. I love you."

"I love you, too."

I hurried out of my room, stopping short when I found people milling about in the hallway. I lowered my eyes and tried to walk past them without saying anything.

"Emery?"

Flip stood against the wall outside his room.

"Are you all right?"

"I think so."

"How about Grady?"

"Do you really care?"

He winced.

I continued walking, desperate to get to the police station. My phone buzzed as soon as I stepped outside. I pulled it out and found a text from Raquel who'd been at her "friend's" dorm all weekend. **What the hell happened?**

She gave me no time to respond. Her next text popped up. **Grady's arrest is all over the Internet.**

My heart sank.

They're saying he'll be off the football team.

Football? I hadn't even considered how it would affect football for him.

God dammit.

Grady

As the nephew of a renowned lawyer, I knew the drill. Let the cops play good cop, bad cop, but say nothing until your lawyer arrived. But I had nothing to hide, so I humored them with brief answers. The moment I mentioned I played football for Alabama, the atmosphere in the interrogation room changed. Both cops started treating me like some over-privileged dickhead who'd purposely beat the shit out of an innocent guy.

"Don't you find it the least bit ironic this guy would show up on a college campus when security there is so tight?" Bad Cop asked.

I cocked my head. "If it were so tight, how'd he get in?"

They exchanged a pissed-off look.

"You said your girlfriend's mom was in the hospital?" Good Cop asked.

I huffed, wanting to get the hell outta there to see Emery and make sure she was okay after everything that went down in her room. I looked from one officer to the other. "You can talk to your superiors. They've been in constant contact with my parents. And you can talk to campus security. They knew Emery was to be checked in on and they knew there was a warrant out for Wayne's arrest."

"We're trying to figure out how this guy shows up at your girlfriend's dorm room when—from what you're telling us—multiple police forces are out looking for him to no avail," Bad Cop said. "And *then*, you beat the hell out of him when you're clearly bigger and he was unarmed."

"Because the unarmed man broke into my girlfriend's room and had her cornered. All of this *after* putting her mother in the hospital. Did you want me to wait for him to pull out a weapon? Maybe sit down and invite him to have dinner with us first?"

Bad Cop slammed his hands down on the table, pushing himself up and leaning into my face. "It's that smug mouth of yours that's gonna bring me pleasure to lock you up."

I shook my head. "I'm tired. And I'm done. My lawyer should be—"

And just like in the movies, my uncle Cal walked in all chill in his charcoal gray suit and green tie. "Don't say another word," he ordered.

I nodded.

He glared at the cops. "If what's been leaked all over the Internet is any indication of how this police department does business, I'll slap you with so many lawsuits your heads will spin."

After some angry phone calls to judges and the district attorney, I was released to my uncle. His hope was Wayne's assault charge against me wouldn't stick. And if it somehow did, because every citizen—even accused felons—had rights, we'd reach an agreement. He had little doubt that this whole fucked-up situation would blow over and be a thing of the past.

"What about Wayne?" I asked Uncle Cal as his driver drove us to my parents' house.

"With a million-dollar bail, he's not going anywhere."

"Thank you," I said, though it didn't seem like enough since he kicked ass back there for me.

"Did you really need to knock the guy out? Your mother's a wreck."

I scrubbed my hands over my face. "When I saw him in there with Emery, something triggered inside me. I snapped. I *wanted* him dead."

"Maybe so, but you can't verbalize that, especially in front of the police." Uncle Cal's phone rang. He checked the screen and looked to me. "I've gotta take this." He lifted it to his ear. "Grady here…" He listened to the caller, his face flushing. "You better tell them we'll sue them for wrongful suspension. We'll create a shit-storm so big they'll be dealing with the aftermath for years."

"What?" I whispered as he unsnapped the briefcase in his lap and shuffled through the papers inside it.

He waved me off and continued his conversation. "I've got the athlete discipline policy right in front of me. I've read it from front to back and there's nothing about an arrest due to self-defense against a wanted man. It's not our fault inaccurate information was leaked to the press before we could self-disclose." He listened to the person on the other end before spewing back, "The teams' PR team needs to do damage control on their end. On our end, he's innocent of any wrongdoing. If they try to bench him, they better believe we're appealing it." He disconnected the call and stewed in the seat beside me. I'd never seen him so fired up. He was known for being calm, cool, and collected. I guess that changed when his nephew was on the chopping block.

"Will I be able to play Saturday against Louisville?"

"I need a minute to process and decide how we'll proceed." He held out his opened palm. "Give me your phone."

"Come on, Uncle Cal."

He leveled me with his courtroom eyes. "You want nothing out there that could be misconstrued or used against you. And the way you kids post everything, I'm not taking any chances."

I placed my phone in his hand, knowing he had my best interest in mind. And regardless of the backlash I received in the press or the misinformation being spread about me, I would have attacked that monster again in a heartbeat if it meant protecting Emery and her mom from him.

It's what I should have done a long time ago.

CHAPTER THIRTY-ONE

Grady

I pounded on Emery's door, probably attracting more attention than I needed. But she didn't answer. Neither did her roommate. Where the hell was she? I didn't want her alone, especially in the room where she'd been attacked. If my uncle hadn't confiscated my phone, I would've already known exactly where she was.

I ran downstairs and hopped in my truck. It had been parked outside her dorm since before I'd been arrested. I drove home, needing a shower to remove the blood still staining my hands.

Dammit.

Reporters, with fucking cameras, lined the sidewalk.

I pulled into the driveway and immediately their lights switched on and the cameras were pointed in my face as I hurried to the door.

"Jordan, can you comment on the attack?" one reporter shouted.

"They're saying your football career's over," another said, trying to get a reaction out of me.

"You think you can handle jail?" another asked as I climbed the front steps and pushed my way inside.

I slammed the door behind me and sat down on the sofa. I sank back into the cushions and covered my head with my arms. "Shit!" I yelled.

"What the hell happened to you?" Abbott asked, entering the room.

I lowered my arms and shook my head in disbelief. "Things got real."

He sat down on the loveseat. "What's that mean?"

"Sorry, man. That's all I'm allowed to say."

"Well, at least tell me if you're okay."

"Awww, were you worried about me, Abbott?"

"Dude, you have no idea the rumors that are spreading around campus."

I shrugged. "Nothing I can do about what people say. I learned that a long time ago."

"There was footage of the guy. *After* you beat him up. Dude, he was a mess."

I shrugged. "He shouldn't have broken into someone's room."

"Those reporters have been here for hours."

"What'd you tell 'em?"

"I didn't answer the door. Girls see that interview and they'd be knocking down the door to see my pretty face."

"Then you'd open your mouth."

He laughed, and I appreciated him trying to make me feel better.

A heavy silence descended before he asked the question we were both thinking. "You gonna be able to play?"

"No idea. My uncle's meeting with the director of intercollegiate athletics first thing in the morning."

"And?"

"Hell if I know."

"Is there anything me and the guys can do to help?"

"Nah. This is all me."

"Coach called a team meeting."

"Yeah?"

"He threatened us. Told us he'd bench our ass if we talked to the media or even each other about you. He said he'd know more tomorrow."

"My uncle was supposed to call him."

"Knowing Coach, he'd rather hear it from you."

I nodded, before pushing myself up. "I'll go see him."

"Woah. What about *her?*"

The lines in my forehead deepened. "Who?"

He ticked his head toward the stairs. "Your girl."

A relieved breath whooshed out of me as I raced up the stairs, two at a time. I froze when I pushed my bedroom door opened and found Em tucked into a ball and asleep on my bed. I could've watched her there forever; she looked so peaceful and safe. But since I knew she was exhausted, and also safe, I figured it would be okay if I slipped out to speak to Coach.

I grabbed a hat off my dresser and pulled it down low. I closed the door softly and crept downstairs. "Don't leave her alone," I ordered Abbott as I snuck out the back door and hopped the neighbor's fence. Coach lived nearby, and the walk would probably serve me well.

Within a few minutes, I stood on the sidewalk outside his house. A single light shined in his first-floor window. I knew he had a wife and son and didn't want to wake them if I rang the doorbell. But if I wanted to play, I needed to talk to the man with the power to make that happen.

I walked up the brick walkway and stopped on his front step. I listened for noise inside—a television maybe—but I heard nothing.

I tapped on the door and waited.

I glanced around at the quiet neighborhood. If I made it to the pros, would I live in a neighborhood like Coach's or a quiet town like the one where I'd grown up?

The door cracked open and Coach stood there in sweats. "Grady?"

"I know it's late, Coach, but I was hoping to speak to you."

He peeked over his shoulder, probably checking to see if I woke up his family. Then he turned back to me and motioned me inside.

I stepped into his entry way as he closed the door behind us.

"Have a seat," he said, walking into a formal living room that looked like it'd never been used.

I followed him and waited to see where he sat. When he sat in a winged-back chair, I sat on the sofa. The firm cushion beneath my ass did little to curb my nerves, but I knew being there was the right thing to do.

"First, let me ask," Coach began. "Are you all right?"

I nodded. "Yeah."

"*Then*, let me ask, are you supposed to be talking to me?"

"No. But I thought it was best you heard the truth from me."

He nodded and didn't say anything else, which was my cue to begin.

"You asked me why I missed those practices a couple weeks ago, and I told you someone close to me was in trouble. You took me at my word and I really appreciated that."

He nodded.

"It was my girlfriend's mother. She was attacked and left for dead."

"What?"

"The man who did it was my girlfriend's estranged stepfather. And he wasn't caught. There's a history of domestic violence with him, and I had a terrible feeling he'd be coming for my girlfriend next. And he did. He followed her to Alabama and broke into her dorm room. He was about to attack her when I showed up."

"Jesus Christ," Coach said, leaning back in his chair and letting my story sink in.

"The guy had the nerve to press charges against me."

Coach rang his hands in front of him, clearly thinking about the repercussions of my actions. "So, where do things stand now legally?"

"My uncle's working on a deal. I'll know more this week. He's also meeting with the director of athletics in the morning."

He nodded, seemingly knowing and understanding what that meant for my future on the football team. His ruling could be anything from community service to dismissal from the team.

"Since the self-disclosure piece was taken away from me with everything being leaked to the media, I wanted you to at least understand what really went down and why."

Coach nodded. "Can I ask you something?"

"Of course."

"If you knew it would ruin your chances at the pros, would you still have done it?"

"Absolutely."

Coach sat silently debating my response.

I stood from the sofa, not wanting to take any more of his time. "Thanks for hearing me out, Coach." I walked toward the front door.

"Grady," he called to me.

I stopped and looked over my shoulder at him still seated in his chair.

"For whatever it's worth, I'll talk to the director myself in the morning."

"Thank you."

"And Grady? You've come a long way this year as a player *and* a human being. I don't want you to think it's gone unnoticed."

My lips twisted in deliberation. "I'm gonna take that as a compliment."

Coach chuckled as I turned and made my way outside his house.

* * *

Thoroughly exhausted after talking to Coach—scratch that—after every fucking thing that had gone down, I pulled off my shirt and shorts and stepped into the shower. Any remnant of blood still on me washed off, and pink water pooled at my feet. Once it had all been washed off, I dried off and walked to my room. I slipped inside quietly, so not to wake Em as I pulled on some boxers. I climbed into bed behind her, wrapping my arms around her small body and trying to lose myself in the familiar scent of her.

"Jordan?" she whispered.

"I'm here."

She twisted in my arms. "Are you okay?"

I dropped my forehead to hers. "Are you seriously asking if I'm okay after what you've been through?"

"You didn't answer my question."

I pulled her closer so I didn't have to lie to her face. "I'm fine. My uncle's working on it."

"I went to the police station. They said you'd been released."

"I'm sorry. We must've just missed you. And Cal confiscated my phone so I couldn't call."

"Doesn't matter. What's gonna happen with football?"

I said nothing partly because I had no clue what would happen behind closed doors.

"Jordan? What's gonna happen?"

"I don't know."

"I won't be able to live with myself if this is what ends your career."

"Em, up until this month, I had no idea a future in football even existed for me. If I lose that opportunity, it was never meant to be anyway."

"Jordan." She pulled back so her eyes met mine. "This is me. Tell me it sucks. Tell me how angry you are. Tell me you blame me for coming back into your life."

"Em." I leveled her with serious eyes. "I would do what I did again in a heartbeat if it meant protecting you."

"Well, I blame *me*."

I pulled her back into me, pressing my lips to the top of her head. "It will all work out," I assured her, though I wondered if it was me I was really trying to convince.

CHAPTER THIRTY-TWO

Grady

I sat on my parents' sofa beside Emery, holding her hand tightly for support while my head hung low. Emery's mom stayed in her room, giving us privacy as we waited for the news from my uncle. My parents sat on the love seat across the room making small talk with Emery, knowing nothing they could say to me would ease my nerves.

"Jordan?" Cal called from the kitchen, having just walked in the side door.

My head whipped up. "In here."

My uncle walked in, greeting all of us before sitting in the corner chair. He folded his hands in front of him and looked me in the eyes. "You're not playing this weekend."

A cold shiver rolled up my spine.

Emery's squeezed me hand, trying to calm what she knew had to be escalating rage inside me.

"When *can* I play?" I asked.

"I'm still working on that," he said.

"Can I stand on the sideline?"

He shook his head. "They don't think it's sending the right message to have you there so soon after being taken into custody."

"What does he need to do?" my father asked.

"Stay out of trouble while I try to work things out on my side," Cal said.

I scoffed. "My record's been clean to this point. I'm not gonna get in any trouble."

"Cal," Emery said softly.

We all looked to her.

"Wayne is a suspected felon who broke into my room. Isn't that breaking and entering? Has that even been discussed? Can't you work that angle?"

"Oddly, your dorm doesn't have cameras on the floors. Only the front and back entrances."

"And?" she persisted.

"And all they saw was someone holding the front door open for him when he presumably asked them to hold it."

"So, right there you have him trespassing," Emery said. "He's not a student. He doesn't have an ID card to get in."

"People visit all the time," my uncle countered.

"He got *inside* my room," she said, her voice rising. "Jordan didn't go looking for a fight."

She was getting angry so I squeezed her hand gently.

"I wish it were that easy," my uncle said. "I've threatened them with every lawsuit under the sun. It's about image. And they want to keep theirs clean. *And* send a message they don't condone violence."

Emery's body tensed.

"It's okay, Em." I assured her, though I was mere seconds away from putting my fist through the nearest wall.

"No, it's not," she said.

I loved her for trying, but it wasn't gonna get me back on the field.

I had a feeling nothing was.

* * *

"You sure you don't wanna come upstairs?" Emery asked once we arrived at her dorm after a silent ride from my parents' house.

"Yeah," I said, my eyes averting hers. "My head's pounding."

She reached over and rested her hand against my cheek. "You know you can talk to me."

I met her gaze. "There's nothing to say."

The sadness in her eyes was impossible to miss, and I hated that I was adding to it. But I was fucking hurting. And trying to wear a brave face for her and everyone else was getting more difficult. I needed to get the hell out of there.

"Tell me you're gonna be okay," she said.

I cocked my head, unable to lie to her.

"I'm so sorry."

"Stop apologizing," I snapped.

She winced and my stomach clenched.

I needed to get out of there before I said anything else I regretted. "I gotta get home."

The pain in her eyes nearly leveled me as she grabbed hold of the door handle. "I'm here if you need me." She pushed open the door and stepped out. From the sidewalk, she stared in at me. She wanted to say something. I could see it in her eyes.

"Good night, Em," I said, wanting her to stop talking and just go inside.

She closed the door and walked to the entrance of her dorm. I knew I didn't have to sit and wait for her to get safely inside since Wayne was in custody, but I did. And once she stepped inside, I pulled away from the curb and sped across campus. I tried to stay strong for her. I really fucking did. But I needed to breathe. And I needed to be alone while I did it.

As soon as I got home, I headed to the basement. I tore off my shirt and spent the next two hours wailing on the punching bag hanging from the ceiling beam. The hardest, head-banging, rock music I could find reverberated off the cement walls around me, pulsing through my veins. Sweat dripped down my face. Red blotches covered my bare chest.

I saw Wayne as I pounded away at the punching bag. I saw everyone I hated in this world. The athletic committee. The police who thought I was guilty. The media who made me look like a crazed lunatic.

I saw fucking red.

Emery

I stood outside Jordan's front door, my knuckles tentatively raised to it. He hadn't called me the previous night. I hadn't expected him to. But since he had no phone, and he hadn't shown up to his morning classes, he left me no choice. He'd stalked me when I arrived on campus. I was returning the favor.

I knocked on the door and rang the doorbell in case music played inside and he couldn't hear me. I turned around, watching students hurrying to their afternoon classes as I waited. I understood why he wouldn't want to attend his classes. I could only imagine the looks and whispers that would surround him. But what would he do at home? I worried the time alone would only hurt him more.

The door swung open.

I twisted around, disappointed to find Jordan's roommate Abbott standing there and not Jordan. "Is he here?"

Abbott didn't make eye contact with me. "No."

I peeked around him inside the house. "Do you know where he is?"

He shifted his hip, as if to block my view. "Nope."

"Do you know when he'll be back?" I asked, peeking around his other side.

He shifted his other hip. "Nope."

"Can I wait?"

His eyes widened. "That's not a good idea."

I crossed my arms and pegged him with my eyes. "Why not?"

"Because…" His eyes lifted, as if searching for the next lie he intended to pull out of thin air. "I've got practice."

I cocked my head. "Do you think I'm gonna steal something?"

"What? No, I just…"

"Listen, I get that he doesn't want to see me. But tell him I'll be back. And when I return, he better be ready to talk to me."

Abbott tucked his guilty lips and said nothing.

I spun away from him and headed back to my dorm knowing what I feared was true. Jordan *did* blame me.

Grady

My fists were numb, but I couldn't stop. I needed this outlet. I needed to get the rage out, just as much as I needed the rock music pounding through my body. It helped the previous night. It needed to keep working or I had no idea what I'd do.

The music switched off.

The only thing I could hear was my panting and the thuds of my fists pounding against the dull leather.

"Enough!"

I stopped punching and turned to see Abbott coming down the basement steps. "What?"

"Go take a shower. You've been down here long enough."

"You my mother now?"

"This isn't helping anything."

I grabbed a towel from a nearby stool and wiped my face. "Says who?"

"Says the guy who doesn't wanna see you break your fingers or wrist."

I swung the towel over my shoulder. "I'm fine. I just needed to get rid of some rage."

"Did you?"

I dragged in a deep breath before shaking my head.

"Why won't you talk to Emery?"

"I don't want her seeing me like this."

"Dude. I've seen you a hundred times worse and I'm still here."

"Yeah, well. I got shit goin' on in my head that I don't want touching her."

"So, you're pushing her away?"

I glared at him. "What's that supposed to mean?"

"Oh, come on. Don't act like you don't keep everyone at arm's length by being a dick most of the time."

I scoffed. "Only most of the time?"

He chuckled. "Less since she's been around."

I rolled my eyes.

"You need her, Grady. Hell, you need me. Don't push us away when you need us the most."

Emery

"Emery."

I lifted my hand to shield my eyes from the early morning sun. I was sitting on a bench outside a small café when Sabrina strode toward me. Her face wore the same concern as mine.

"How is he?" she asked as she sat down beside me. "My calls keep going straight to voicemail."

"His uncle took his phone."

She nodded, now understanding why he hadn't answered his phone.

"If it helps, he's not talking to me either."

"I'm sorry," she said.

I lifted my shoulders.

"Do you know what happened? Is he all right?"

I found it difficult to hold her gaze. "He was protecting me from my stepfather."

"Oh my God. He found you?" Her eyes assessed me, looking for visible scars. "Are you all right?"

I nodded. "So, Jordan told you about my past?"

She cringed. "I haven't told a soul. I promise. He just needed someone to talk to when you showed up on campus."

"It's fine. I'm glad he had you to talk to."

"Yeah, but who does he have now if he's shutting us out?" she asked.

A silence passed between us.

"The press is making it out to look like he's a loose cannon who went looking for a fight," she said.

I closed my eyes for a long moment, unable to hide my regret. "I know."

"What about football?" she asked.

I shook my head, wondering if this was the moment it would occur to her that *I* was the reason Jordan's life had been turned upside down.

"He must be devastated."

I nodded. "But I think I know how you can help."

* * *

I awoke to a dark room. My phone vibrated on the nightstand beside my head. My heart raced as I reached over and grabbed it. The time read two o'clock and an unfamiliar number lit up the screen. I tapped on the screen and lifted the phone to my ear, whispering so not to wake Raquel. "Hello?"

It was silent on the other end.

A shiver rushed through me. "Hello?" I repeated.

"Em?" Jordan said.

I pulled in a sharp breath. "Jordan. Are you okay?"

"Yeah."

Knowing better than to apologize to him yet again, I said the only thing I could in that moment. "I miss you."

Silence.

Shit. "Did you need something?" I asked, treading carefully.

There was a long pause before he spoke. "Just wanted to hear your voice."

Pained by his words, I closed my eyes tightly. "You can call me any time."

Silence.

I didn't want to push him, but I needed him to know I was there for him. "Will I see you soon?"

There was another long pause before he spoke. "Good night, Em."

Dammit.

It took everything in me, but I willed back the tears that were ready to fall as I sat with the phone to my ear, knowing he'd hung up.

CHAPTER THIRTY-THREE

Grady

I told myself not to watch. I tried to stay distracted. But right at kick-off time, I switched on the game.

I needed to see if we kicked the shit out of Louisville.

With each passing minute, I moved closer toward the television as if I could actually reach through the screen and block for Flip who'd been sacked twice in the first half. I wanted to clear a path for our running back who found no way through Louisville's defense.

At halftime, we were down by two touchdowns. I switched off the television. I didn't like watching us lose, especially without me there. I wanted my team to look good out there despite my absence. Down deep, though, I knew they needed me.

I stared at the ceiling as I lay in my silent room. I wished Emery was there with me. Abbott had been right. I did need her. And I had been less of a dick since she showed up on campus. But I didn't want anyone with me as I stewed over not being able to play. I didn't want her to see that side of me. She always looked at me like I could do anything—be anything. I didn't want the pussy I felt like inside marring her vision of me.

That was the *last* thing I wanted to happen.

* * *

Abbott slammed the front door when he arrived home a few hours later. He was pissed. He should've been. The team sucked out there. The kitchen cabinets opened and closed with the same amount of force. He wasn't only pissed, but he was hungry after the loss—and inescapable reaming out by Coach.

It became quiet. Abbott must've settled down on the sofa to watch the other college games like we usually did together after our home games. He knew better than to check if I'd be joining him. He knew enough to leave me alone until I felt like talking.

"Dude!" Abbott shouted from downstairs.

The fuck?

"You need to get down here!"

I didn't budge from my bed. "No!"

"Dude! You need to get your ass down here right *now*!"

"What the fuck?" I grumbled as I pushed myself up and swung my bare feet off the side of my bed. "I swear to God," I called to him. "If this is some lame-ass attempt to cheer me up, you and me, we're gonna throw down."

"Hurry up!" he persisted.

Begrudgingly, I dragged my ass downstairs.

Abbott sat on the sofa with the remote pointed at the television. "You gotta see this."

He had paused whatever it was he was watching, then hit play as I sat down next to him.

"These videos have been popping up all over social media today," the sports broadcaster on the screen said as a video of Caden Brooks played.

"I'm Caden Brooks and I stand against domestic violence."

The next video played and Trace Forester's face filled the screen. "I'm Trace Forester and I stand against domestic violence and those who commit heinous acts against women and children."

Sabrina's boyfriend appeared in the next video. "I'm Crosby Parks and I say no-freaking-way to domestic abuse and any violence against women."

I was stunned as I watched professional athlete after professional athlete share similar messages about domestic violence.

"I guess these athletes are trying to send a message to the powers that be down in Alabama, where offensive tackle Jordan Grady was recently suspended due to an alleged assault against his girlfriend's abusive stepfather." The broadcaster smirked. "Well done, gentlemen. Message received."

"Holy shit," I said, my mouth hanging open. "What the hell was that?"

Abbott grinned. "I'd say that was your ticket back to the team."

Emery

There was a knock on my door. It was so nice not having to worry about who might be on the other side when I opened it. I stood up from my bed where I'd been studying in my pajamas and opened the door.

Jordan lunged forward.

I gasped as he wrapped his arms around me and buried his nose in my hair.

"Thank you," he said as he kicked the door shut and walked us into my room.

Elation swept over my body as I let him hold me, rejoicing in the feel of him. It had been *days* since I'd seen him. Since I felt his touch. Since I knew he wanted to see me.

He pulled back, but only enough to see me. "I know what you did."

"What *Sabrina* and I did," I corrected him.

He laughed before capturing my lips and kissing me long and hard.

God. I missed this.

He eventually pulled away, leaving me breathless and undoubtedly flushed. "How the hell am I ever gonna repay you?"

"Stop pushing me away."

"Done."

I chuckled at the matter-of-fact way he said it.

"Anything else?" he asked.

My lips twisted as I thought for a moment. "You told me Em's your new best friend. But I've been thinking. I really want to be your old best friend again."

He considered my request with a small grin. "Done."

"Oh, and last one, I promise."

"Okay," he said skeptically.

"Never *ever* doubt that I'd do anything for you. Because I love you, Jordan Grady."

The coolest smirk I'd ever seen spread across his lips. "I love *you*, Emery Pruitt." He leaned in and kissed me slow and gently, pulling away much too soon. "Now, I'm gonna need you to say that again so I'm ready for it this time."

I laughed. "I love you—"

His mouth cut me off before I could finish my words. He lowered me down onto my bed, his body pressing me into the mattress as his kiss conveyed his appreciation.

Had he *just* realized I loved him and would do anything for him? Hadn't he been paying attention?

His hands dropped to the hem of my shirt. He pulled back from my lips and ripped my shirt over my head, tossing it to the floor. He gazed down at me in my pajama shorts and pink bra. "God, I love looking at you like this." He leaned back down and his mouth captured mine, his tongue diving in, possessive and determined.

Though it was the last thing I wanted to do, I pushed at his chest, trying to get him off me. "Raquel could be back any minute."

"I don't care. I need to be inside you."

My belly dipped. I loved when he talked to me that way—probably because I never imagined I'd ever be on the receiving end of it. I'd wished. Oh, how I'd wished. But the reality was so much sweeter—and dirtier.

My hands moved to the waist of his shorts. My attempt to push them down and over his ass was futile.

He reached down and assisted, tossing his shorts to the floor. "I've really missed you."

We both snapped our heads to the door when we heard movement outside. It had to be Raquel.

"Go away!" Jordan shouted.

"You've got an hour!" Raquel shouted back through the door. "*If* it's not over in two minutes, Grady!"

"Fuck off!" he shouted to her.

I giggled as her footsteps disappeared down the hallway.

Jordan reached behind his head and pulled off his shirt.

I'd never get sick of seeing *him* that way. Instinctively, I lifted my hands to his chest. My fingertips trailed over his smooth skin, tracing the ridges in his abs. He closed his eyes, apparently enjoying my exploration as much as

I was. My fingers drifted to his pecs. My thumbs circled his nipples. His eyes closed tighter. My fingertips coasted up until I cupped the stubble on his chin and cheeks. "Jordan."

His eyes opened.

"I'm ready."

That must've been what he'd been waiting for. He pushed my shorts down my legs and tossed them across the room. He scooted down my body, urged my legs apart, and disappeared between them.

Holy shit.

His warm mouth landed between my thighs. I squeezed my eyes shut as his tongue darted out, tracing a long hard lick up the seam of my body. *Holy. Shit.* I panted louder than I thought possible as he did it again and again. "*Jordan.*"

"Got you, babe. No worries."

His lips closed over my clit and he sucked. *Hard.* I pulled in a sharp breath. *Sweet Jesus.* He added his tongue and circled it. Around and around. *Oh, God.* When my panting wasn't enough to show him how much I loved what he was doing to me, he lapped at my clit.

My head pushed back into the bed as my hands grasped at his shoulders. I didn't know if I wanted to keep him right where he was or push him off me. Sensations swirled. My clit throbbed.

Oh. My. God.

He abandoned my clit, leaving me gasping for air as if I'd just run a marathon. I groaned my displeasure.

"Not done," he murmured between my legs. His tongue returned, swiping along my folds in a slow, torturous path. He stopped on my clit and swirled his tongue around it, flicking it again and again. Then he repeated. Swipe. Swirl. Flick.

That was it.

My legs trembled.

My core coiled.

And all at once, tremors exploded, rippling out to the tips of my toes and fingertips.

Oh. My. Freaking. God.

I could barely catch my breath as the tremors began to subside and a warm buzz radiated from every pore in my body. I lay there with my heart racing, reveling in the numbness sweeping over me.

Jordan kept at it, milking my body for all he could until I lay limp and satiated. He finally stopped torturing me and kissed his way up my body until he covered me with his.

"I had no idea something like that was even possible," I admitted, half-drunk on what he'd done to me.

He snickered.

"Can we do it again?" I asked.

"And again. And again."

Jordan made good on his promise, making my body quake in the most delicious ways over and over again that night. Raquel must've realized we needed time alone because she didn't return until the next morning.

Smart girl.

CHAPTER THIRTY-FOUR

Grady

I walked into the locker room to the applause and cheers of my teammates. I looked over my shoulder out the doorway, pretending I didn't know it was all for me. But when I turned back, they all greeted me with pats on the back and hugs.

"Welcome back, dude," Rivers said.

"Hasn't been the same without you," Hayes assured me.

"They mean it hasn't been as loud without you," Abbott shouted from nearby.

The guys laughed. And though I laughed with them, it hadn't been easy waiting for the athletic board to reverse their decision *or* the charges against me to be dropped. Wayne thought it would help in his sentencing if he agreed to drop them. But it didn't. A first-degree attempted murder charge carried a life sentence. He copped a plea deal that ensured him the *possibility* of parole. Hopefully, he died in prison before we ever had to worry about that.

"All right, all right," Coach said, entering the crowded room. "Nice to have you back, Grady." His eyes shot around at my teammates. "Now let's get back to business. You all sucked on Saturday. You better turn it around this week because Texas is tough."

I sat down on the stool in front of my locker and drew a deep breath as Coach reamed us out for the next fifteen minutes. But truth be told. I was so damn happy to be reamed out. To be back in the locker room I'd called home for four seasons. To be surrounded by the guys. To have my shot at proving myself worthy of the pros again.

Coach ran our asses into the ground at practice. An hour in, I was ready to collapse. I dropped down onto the sideline bench and squirted a stream of cold water down my throat.

"Nice to have you back."

I lowered the bottle and met Flip's eyes. "Is it?"

He looked down at his cleats. "Listen. We need to talk."

"Then talk."

"Not here. After practice."

My eyes narrowed. What the hell was going on? He wouldn't even look at me. "All right," I agreed, more out of curiosity than anything else.

"I'll meet you out front after practice." He turned away from me and jogged back out onto the field. He said nothing else to me. Even when he called plays in the huddle, he didn't once look at me.

After practice ended, I stayed in the shower a lot longer than usual. My muscles needed relief and the hot water cascading over me was a welcome pain reliever. When I stepped into the locker room after, it was deserted, except for Coach in his office. I dressed and grabbed my bag. Before heading out, I glanced around at the locker room one last time, so damn happy I'd been allowed back. I guess I really didn't know what I had until it was being torn away from me. Now I knew, and I'd fight tooth and nail to hold onto it.

"Grady." Flip leaned against the brick wall as I stepped outside the building.

"Talk," I said, not bothering to stop as I made my way across the parking lot toward my truck.

"I want to apologize."

I balked. "Yeah? Why's that?"

"Because I came in here an overconfident dick and you saw right through me."

I clicked the button on my keys to unlock the door. "I'm not buying it." I turned to face him, but his eyes were again on everything but me. "What aren't you saying?"

He dropped his head back and closed his eyes. "I let that guy into Emery's room."

"Come again?"

"It was me. I knew her passcode. And I let him in."

My bag slipped from my hand as rage coursed through my body. My limbs shook. All I saw was red. All I wanted to do was rip his fucking head off. I stepped toward him, ready to throw down.

He held up his hands. "Let me explain," he begged, his voice reaching a high pitch.

"He said he was her stepdad and wanted to surprise her," he said in one frantic breath, clearly seeing the anger radiating off of me.

My fists clenched at my sides. "Like hell he did."

"But I didn't know that. I knew she was pissed at me and I thought I could make it up to her by helping with her surprise."

"How you feeling about that now, motherfucker?"

He backed up, his hands up once again, so feeble and scared. "Listen. I know you wanna kick the shit outta me. But this is killing me. My part in what went down. I deserve it. I deserve whatever I have coming."

I stopped, trying like hell to rein in my anger. I knew I didn't need any more trouble, but I was so fucking pissed I needed to hurt him.

"He's behind bars now," he continued, pleading his case. "And she's okay."

"You're really trying to justify this?"

He shook his head. "All I'm saying is, it all worked out in the end."

A sardonic laugh shot out of me. "So, you're looking for thanks?"

"No, man. I just needed you to know the truth."

"Why? So, your conscious is clean?"

"So, we can start over. I need you as much as you need me this year. And somehow that got fucked up."

"*You* fucked it up," I assured him.

"I did. And I'm taking the blame. Just tell me what I can do to make everything right?"

I thought long and hard. I hated him. That I knew for sure. And when I hated someone, I usually never got over that shit. But he was right. I needed him to make me look good out there. And if I learned anything during this whole ordeal, it's people are stronger as a unit. Nothing good comes from working against other people. The guys had single-handedly gotten me back on the team without resorting to evil methods. They chose a way that would enlighten and help the cause Emery would one day pledge her life to helping.

So, what were my options?

Embarrass him?

Make him do my dirty work?

Or even better…

"Fine," I said. "I know what you can do for me—and Em."

CHAPTER THIRTY-FIVE

Emery

Raquel had lent me her car, which was a lifesaver since Jordan was nowhere to be found. The big game was that weekend, so I knew he was preoccupied.

I drove off campus, pulling down the visor to protect my eyes from the brutal setting sun as I drove through town. My mom was moving into her new place the following day, and I promised to go shopping with her to help decorate to make her condo feel like home.

The sun had set by the time I pulled onto my old street and parked in the Gradys' driveway. I hurried up to the door, knocking once on the side door to let them know I was there. I stepped inside the kitchen. "Hello?"

"In the living room," my mother called.

I made my way through the kitchen and into the living room. My mom sat in the corner chair while Mr. and Mrs. Grady sat on the sofa. "Hi."

They all greeted me.

"You ready to go?" I asked my mom.

My mother smiled. "I changed my mind. I think I've got everything I need."

I let out an incredulous laugh. "You do, huh? Why didn't you call me then?"

They all smiled, almost *too* happy I'd driven from campus for no reason.

"Am I missing something?" I asked, feeling like I was the last one to the party.

"Maybe," Mrs. Grady said as she stood from the sofa and wrapped her arm around my shoulders. "Come with me."

I glanced to my mother as Mrs. Grady led me out of the living room and to the back door. I stilled as soon as I saw it. My insides became light and airy. "It's so beautiful," I whispered as I took in the tiny white lights twinkling like stars in the big tree out back.

"It's for you," she said.

My head shot to her. "For me?"

She lifted her chin toward the tree and pushed open the door. "Go out there."

I stepped outside, the cool night air prickling the skin on my arms. I glanced back and realized she wasn't following me out.

"Go ahead," she urged.

I turned back to the tree and made my way over to it. It was beautiful before it had been filled with lights. Now it was exquisite. I stood under the long branches and looked up. The only thing I could see were lights. Thousands of lights creating a magical canopy. A wonderland. A place I never wanted to leave.

Huh. That was exactly the way I'd felt about Jordan's house when I was growing up.

Music began playing softly. Instantly, I recognized the song. Jordan had played it when we danced under the same tree so long ago.

My head swung around, knowing he had to be nearby.

He stepped out from behind the large trunk wearing khaki pants and a white button-down shirt. He looked gorgeous—the way he always had in my eyes.

"What are you doing?" I asked.

He walked over to me with a smirk, kissing me soft

and slow. He pulled back, leaving me breathless. "I will never get sick of doing that."

My eyes flashed up to the lights above us. "This looks beautiful."

"It was time."

My face wore my confusion. Time? Time for what?

"You told me on our first date that you would follow me anywhere. Did you mean that?"

I tilted my head. "Do you even have to ask that?"

He nodded. "Yup. I need to know."

"Of course I'd follow you anywhere. I've been doing it since we met, haven't I?"

His smile turned my insides mushy. Every time.

I watched as he slowly lowered himself down onto one knee.

Oh. My. God.

He pulled out a small box and looked up at me. "I know we're young and we have our whole lives ahead of us…"

I clasped my hand over my mouth.

"But there's not another person in this world I'd want to be on this journey with. I don't want you following me anymore, Emery. I want you right by my side. I love you more than I ever thought possible. I know you may want to wait until you graduate and open your shelter, but I need to put a ring on your finger so I'll know, without a shadow of a doubt, that you'll be mine forever."

Tears tumbled out of my eyes and down my cheeks. "I've always been yours," I assured him.

His lips quirked in the corners. "I'm gonna need a more definitive answer. It's good for the ego, you know."

I laughed through my tears. "Yes. Yes. *Yes.*"

His smile reached his eyes as he opened the box and pulled out a diamond ring. The stone sparkled almost as brilliantly as the lights above us.

I held out my shaking hand and he slipped the ring onto my finger. I didn't even look at it. I was too taken by the way he stared up at me with the kind of happiness only attainable when you found "The One."

Jordan pushed himself to his feet and lifted me right off mine. I wrapped my legs around his hips and our lips collided. I was marrying Jordan Grady. I'd told him a long time ago we'd get married someday. He didn't believe me back then. But I'd been right. I'd been right all along.

When Jordan pulled away, I was breathless as usual and floating on cloud nine. "Let's go show our parents," he said.

I laughed, loving his enthusiasm. He placed me down and grabbed hold of my hand as we walked toward our parents, who were all smiling in the doorway.

A light shining in a nearby bush caught my attention. "What's that?"

Jordan glanced to where I peered into the darkness. "Oh, that's just Flip."

My voice squeaked incredulously. "Flip?"

"Yeah. I needed someone to record the moment. Figured Flip was the best one for the job."

Leave it to Jordan to make his point clear. I threw back my head and laughed then stopped completely, holding Jordan back with me. I reached up and pulled his mouth down to mine and kissed him. He wasn't the only one happy to drive the point home to Flip. I was Jordan's girl. Always had been. Always would be.

FINALLY
Three Years Later

Emery

I pulled in a deep breath, feeling calmer than I'd ever felt in my life. Why wouldn't I? My dream was about to come true in front of the people I cared most for in this world.

"You ready?" my mom asked.

I glanced over my shoulder. She stood there in a beautiful purple dress. You'd never know she'd once endured such trauma. Her wounds had healed. The sparkle in her eyes had returned. So had her smile.

I had my mom back.

"Yes. I'm ready." I stood from the stool in front of Mrs. Grady's dresser. My strapless, fitted, white dress hung to the floor and covered my bare feet. My veil, with its edges steeped with sparkles, hung down my back covering my hair, which was curled in flowing waves.

"You look breathtaking," my mom said as I stepped beside her and kissed her cheek.

"Thanks, Mama." I walked through the Grady's empty house until I stood in the door, gazing out at the yard aglow with sunshine—the way I always remembered my childhood. Only a few chairs filled the lawn area beneath the tree. We both wanted to keep the ceremony small. The Gradys sat beside Uncle Cal. Sabrina, Crosby, and Abbott sat behind them. Raquel and Vanessa, my friend from Arizona, sat across the aisle beside an empty chair for my mom.

My eyes moved from them to the one person I really sought.

Jordan, wearing a black suit, was speaking to Father Hall, who had been our priest when we were kids. Jordan's back faced everyone. Professional football looked good on him. His arms were rock hard, and he'd kept off the weight. I was so proud of the way he'd taken over as a leader so quickly on his team. He had the respect of his teammates and the coaching staff. And people were beginning to take notice of him as a real threat on the field. And, though I'd just finished my senior year, I'd made it to every one of his games. Because when I promised Jordan Grady I'd do something, I always made good on that promise.

"It's time," my mom said as she pushed open the door and stepped outside.

I followed her, slipping my arm through hers as we moved across the yard toward the tree.

Soft music began to play.

Everyone stood.

Jordan finally turned. He pulled in a sharp breath as a huge smile spread across his face.

And, in that moment, it was as if everyone else just disappeared. And all I saw was Jordan. Always Jordan.

My mom and I stopped once we reached him. She released my arm and hugged him. "Be good to her," she whispered.

"You know I will," he assured her.

She stepped away and sat beside Raquel and Vanessa.

Jordan took my hands in his big bear claws. "Hi."

"Hi," I said, trying to suppress the grin that fought to take over every part of my face.

"You look—" we both said, laughing at our sudden awkwardness.

"You look beautiful," he said.

My cheeks warmed, never immune to the power of his words. "You do too."

"Well, Sabrina said I look hot," he teased.

"I'm never living that down," she mumbled from her chair behind us.

I laughed as I glanced toward her. "Can you stop boosting his already massive ego?"

She rolled her eyes and shook her head.

I looked back to Jordan. "I think you look hot too."

"Obviously."

"Should we begin?" Father Hall asked.

I nodded with a grin.

"Father, the shorter you make this ceremony," Jordan said. "The sooner I get to hold my wife."

My belly rippled at the sound of 'wife' rolling off Jordan's tongue. I was minutes away from being Jordan Grady's wife. *Mrs.* Jordan Grady.

Holy. Freaking. Cow.

"We are gathered here today to join this man and this woman in holy matrimony," Father Hall began, his voice a bit shaky with age.

I stared into Jordan's eyes, remembering every important moment we'd shared. He was my first everything. The first boy I kissed. The first boy I slept with. The first boy I loved—the only boy I loved. Those moments, and so many others, were engrained in my brain and heart forever.

As Father Hall continued with our brief ceremony, Jordan's blue eyes gazed at me. Someday our children would have the same blue gaze. Because we *would* have children. And they'd be as outgoing, funny, and loving as Jordan. And hopefully as strong, committed, and passionate as me.

Father Hall's voice broke through my thoughts. "Do you, Emery Pruitt, take Jordan Grady to be your lawfully wedded husband? Do you promise to be faithful to him in good times and bad, in sickness and in health, and to love and to honor him all the days of your life?"

Jordan's eyes riveted between mine, as if he didn't already know my answer.

"I do," I said, my heartbeat quickening.

Father Hall looked to Jordan. "Do you—"

"I do," Jordan said.

Everyone laughed.

"You have to let him finish," I whispered.

His thumbs brushed over the backs of my hands. "Fine."

Father Hall tried again. "Do you, Jordan Grady, take Emery Pruitt to be your lawfully wedded wife? Do you promise to be faithful to her in good times and bad, in sickness and in health and to love and to honor her all the days of your life?"

"Oh, hell, yes!"

Everyone laughed.

Jordan's eyes shot to Father Hall. "Sorry, Father."

Father Hall winked at him.

"Can I kiss her now?" Jordan asked.

"Not yet," Father Hall said. "Do you have the rings?"

Jordan dug into his pocket and pulled out my ring.

I turned to my mom who handed me Jordan's wedding band.

Father Hall blessed the rings and then looked to Jordan. "Jordan, repeat after me. Emery, I give you this ring as a symbol of my love."

Jordan held a beautiful diamond wedding band between his thumb and index finger and slipped it onto my extended ring finger as he said, "Emery, I give you this ring as a symbol of my love."

I stared down at the exquisite ring on my finger. Jordan had picked it out on his own and wouldn't let me see it. I glanced up at him. "It's beautiful."

He smiled as he eagerly held out his hand.

I held his band between my fingers. "Jordan, I give you this ring as a symbol of my love." I slipped the ring onto his ring finger.

Jordan smiled. "I hope you give me babies, too. Lots of them."

Everyone laughed again.

Jordan glanced to Father Hall. "Now, Father?"

Father Hall shook his head with amusement in his eyes. "One more thing. It is with great pleasure, before your family and friends, that I pronounce you husband and wife. *Now*, you may kiss your bride."

"My wife," Jordan whispered, before lifting me right off my feet and kissing me.

Applause and laughter surrounded us, but all I saw was Jordan.

My husband.

EPILOGUE
One Year Later

Emery

A lump formed in my throat as I stood behind the door, waiting to see all the smiling faces. My mama stood beside me, her hand gripping mine like a vice. I knew she didn't like to be the center of attention, but I couldn't think of anyone I wanted by my side in this moment more than I wanted her.

The doors opened and we stepped out, greeted by a round of applause. I glanced to Jordan standing behind a podium, having just introduced us to the attendees. He walked over and kissed my mom on the cheek before pulling me into his muscular arms. "I love you," he whispered. "And I'm so proud of you."

I smiled, trying to push my nerves aside as he moved me to the podium. I looked out at the sea of women sitting there. So many of them had escaped difficult lives and the abusive men who had made it that way. They finally had a place to call home until we could find them a new place. A new job. A new happiness.

"Thank you," I said into the clump of microphones, waiting for their applause to subside. "This is a true dream come true for me. It's what I've dreamt about since my mother and I escaped an abusive home and didn't know where to go to start over."

I glanced to my mama. Tears glazed her eyes. She was so proud of what Jordan and I had created. So very proud.

"If we were able to escape our situation, then I am confident that any woman who finds herself in a situation that is unsafe or unhealthy can too."

I looked into the television cameras in the back of the room. Thanks to Jordan's appearance, along with a few of his teammates, we had quite the turnout and media coverage. "To any woman out there who knows she doesn't deserve the life she's living. To any woman out there who is scared from the moment she wakes up until the moment she goes to bed. To any woman who wants better for not only herself but for her children too. There is a place for you. A *safe* place. Here at The Safety Net, we want to help you. No. We *will* help you."

The room burst into applause and Jordan stepped up beside me, wrapping his arms around me. When our gazes met, I saw so much in his eyes—love, pride, happiness. I smiled. Jordan had been *my* safety net. I wanted nothing more than to give that to women out there who didn't have a Jordan Grady to catch them. Luckily, I had him, and I'd never let him go again.

THE END

If you or someone you love is in need of assistance, there is help available.
National Domestic Violence Hotline
1-800-799-7233
http://www.thehotline.org/

OTHER TITLES BY J. NATHAN

If you enjoyed Grady and Emery's story, check out
the other standalones in the *For You* series:
For Finlay (Book #1 Caden & Finlay's story)
For Forester (Book #2 Trace's story)
For Crosby (Book #3 Sabrina's story)

Savage Beasts Rock Star Standalone Series
Kozart
Treyton

Standalones
Seren
Something About You
I Just Need You
You're the Reason
Until Alex
Since Drew
Before Hadley

ACKNOWLEDGEMENTS

Thank you so much for taking the time to read Grady and Emery's story. I hope you enjoyed it as much as I enjoyed writing it! I hope I did all you Grady fans proud.

To all the bloggers and readers who have continued to spread the word about my books. I cannot tell you how much I appreciate you. Without you, no one would be reading my books. Thank you so very much!!!!

To my wonderful beta readers: Dali, Neilliza, Suzanne, Megan, Renee, Kim, Kerrie, and Heather. Thank you for taking the time to read *For Emery* when it wasn't at its best. Your feedback is *always* appreciated. Do not think for a single second that I do not know how very lucky I am to have all of you supporting me. Thank you!!!

To my editor Stephanie Elliot. Thank you for always giving it to me straight and for fixing words like *eyes*, *dropped*, *smile*, *blonde*, and *all right*. Maybe by book ten I will have them down! LOL!

To my PA Renee. Thank you for all you do, and for giving me honest feedback but tempering it with lots of glitter gifs. I appreciate your insight and assistance with…everything. Please know I'd be lost without you!

To Letitia at RBA Designs for creating yet another beautiful cover. Thank you!

And last, but certainly not least, to my husband and son. Thank you for your support. Honey, I could not do this if you didn't take soccer practice duty half the time to give me the time to write. You know I love writing, but you two always come first.

ABOUT THE AUTHOR

J. Nathan resides on the east coast with her husband and soon to be nine-year-old son. She is an avid reader of all things romance. Happy endings are a must. Alpha males with chips on their shoulders are an added bonus. When she's not curled up with a good book, she can be found spending time with family and friends and working on her next novel.